BY DENNIS HASELEY

GETTING HIM

GETTING HIM

DENNIS HASELEY

Farrar Straus Giroux   New York

Published simultaneously in Canada by HarperCollins*CanadaLtd*
Printed in the United States of America
Designed by Amy Samson
First edition, 1994

Library of Congress Cataloging-in-Publication Data
Haseley, Dennis.
Getting him / Dennis Haseley.—1st ed.
p.   cm.
[1. Revenge—Fiction.   2. Family problems—Fiction.]   I. Title.
PZ7.H2688Ge 1994 [Fic]—dc20 94-6421 CIP AC

GETTING HIM

ONE

Anyone will tell you that the thing that made the 1956 Buick unique was the four holes along the side. It was the second-to-last year they did it; but it was probably the last good year for Buicks. It may have had the same frame as a Chevy, but those four marks lifted it to another class. Even Keith would have admitted it, even Jim would have—if Jim let himself talk about things like that. I used to think it gave the car a space-age look—didn't rockets have holes like that as well? But I would never be caught admitting it, because it was Harold's family that had the 1956 sky-blue Buick Roadmaster with whitewall tires.

Across the street and down a little ways, it was parked in his driveway. And Harold was sitting in it.

I could see him from my bedroom window. I was supposed to be doing my math homework, but instead I was going through my mother's coins. She and I had a deal that I could look through her change and keep those pennies I needed for my collection, if I would put them in rolls when I was finished, so she could take them to the bank. From there, I guessed, they ended up in circulation and eventually back in my mother's possession, for me to go through again. Even though I rarely found a penny I didn't already have, I always checked. They were spread out in front of me now—the pennies from her coin purse, the others pressed in my collection book.

Harold had been sitting in the Buick for about forty-five minutes—through a taut moment when I thought the D on a 1955 cent was really an S; through a whole group of boring, shiny 1957 and new 1958 pennies; through the finding of a steel 1943 penny—made during the war—which I already had, but put aside anyway.

Harold's mother had come out and was standing beside the driver's window. She was gesturing with her hands, so I could tell she was talking to him. It was a late February day, cold, with breezes blowing off Lake Erie. She'd already gone into the house once and gotten a coat and a scarf for her head.

The paperboy glided up on his three-speed bike, and I could imagine the *tick tick tick* sounding from his rear wheel. He was a Boy Scout, several years older than me, named Richard Kenny. He stood by his bike with a rolled-up newspaper in his hand, and turned from Harold's mother to the kid in the driver's seat. Harold was pretty small. I could just see the round blond top of his head behind the steering wheel, or maybe it was only a melon balanced on top of a bag of groceries.

I would need to take a closer look.

My mother was sitting in the living room. I watched her for a moment from the hallway: she was sewing curtains from a pattern book. As she inserted and pulled out the needle, she seemed to be quietly speaking to someone who wasn't there.

I cleared my throat and walked in.

"I want to go out for a little while," I said.

"Okay, then." She placed her finger on the diagram; they were curtains for my room, with different kinds of sailboats on them.

"Is it okay if I take Chief?"

She nodded and gave me a smile. Then she looked down again at the pattern in the book.

Chief seemed glad to see me. I felt sorry for him sometimes, when I looked out the back window at him chained to his little house. I supposed there was a secret language that he and the birds and squirrels knew, and that they taunted him for being a big black-and-white dog who had invaded their world and was now imprisoned there, in a kind of solitary confinement. There was also his name, Chief. When my father brought him from the kennel as a puppy, he had said, "Here's your Dalmatian." And when the puppy ran to me, my father called "Chief!" sharply, and the dog stopped and looked at him. My father nodded. "You know. A firehouse dog."

"It's a good name," I had said.

I unhooked him from the chain and clicked his collar to the end of the leash I carried. I often wished we could keep him in the house, but he made my father jumpy. When Chief would go to lie down at night in the living room, he would turn around and around in a circle—as if he was trampling down weeds, as ancient wild dogs must have learned to do. My father couldn't read his newspaper until the dog settled down. And then Chief would bark. Or yawn. Or get up to find a better spot. And my father would go out into the kitchen to get a second beer. Finally, my mother had told me we couldn't keep him in the house. "He makes too much racket," she had said. But I knew "racket" was a word she never used.

We crossed the street and he was straining at the leash. He loved to run. He would always try to jump out of the window of the car when my father and I took him to the park. My father seemed to enjoy it there, smoking his cigarette while that dog tore around us in huge circles.

There was a little crowd now around the 1956 Buick. Richard Kenny was still stationed by his bicycle, the Friday papers from half his route bulging from the saddlebags. Harold's mother had given up talking to her son and was standing several paces off, staring into the distance. Mrs. Miller, a lady who lived next door to Harold's family and who always seemed to be dressed in a bathrobe—even in the middle of winter you would see its pink hem hanging beneath her winter coat when she brought in the mail—was shaking her head.

"He won't come out," she said to me, and then looked to Harold's mother, who seemed to ignore her.

Mrs. Miller turned to Richard and said, "You'd think they'd have another key."

"His dad has another set," said Harold's mother tightly. "But he's not on the lot."

I had never been this close to Harold's mother before, and she was younger than I would have imagined. She had blond hair under her scarf, and red lipstick that seemed brighter, perhaps, because of the gray February day. If it weren't for the lines around her eyes, I could have thought she was in high school.

I walked along the sky-blue metal, past the extra chrome strip on the door. I walked toward those four cool holes in the front fender and then I stopped and glanced in the window. Harold was sitting in the driver's seat with his head tilted down, not looking at anyone. There was a determined expression on his face. A golf hat—yellow, with crossed clubs on the front—was on the seat next to him. The keys were dangling in the ignition.

My arm yanked. Chief had discovered a smell under one of the bushes bordering the driveway. I jiggled the leash to calm him down, and when that didn't work, I walked him back to where we'd been standing. There, he developed a strong interest in Mrs. Miller's bathrobe, so I brought him up short, and he started panting and gagging.

"Is he trying to drive somewhere?" I asked, which no one seemed to find a helpful addition. I let Chief's leash out a little, and he yawned and sat down.

Harold's mother shook her head and took a step toward the car. She looked at Harold—her reflection wavy in the glass—and then back at me.

"Donald," she said. "That's right, isn't it? Donald, maybe you could talk to him."

Mrs. Miller and Richard Kenny turned their faces toward me. I was going to say something to Richard about how he should try to win a merit badge for this—a little silver car—but instead just cleared my throat. We were all still for a moment, the way Harold was inside the Buick. Then Chief yanked at my arm.

"I'll just tie him up," I said. I walked around to the other side of the car. The bushes there would never hold him, and I didn't want him pulling over Richard Kenny's bike. I looked over at Harold's mother through the glass and held up the leash to the passenger-side door handle and she nodded her head. I looped the leash there, and told Chief to stay, and then walked around to the driver's side window.

"Harold," I said through the window. "Now, listen." I glanced at Harold's mother: two lines had set in around her mouth.

I moved forward, so I was staring at him through the corner of the front windshield.

"Come on," I said. "Everybody's waiting." It seemed as if he couldn't hear me, as if he wasn't sitting in a parked Buick, but was some intrepid pilot, sticking to his course in the darkness of the upper sky. "Come on and open the door," I said, but I could tell he wouldn't.

Then there was a sound like a blow, and a sudden white shape on the other window. I jumped back and saw it was Chief, his face against the glass like a frightful black-and-white mask. He must have been jumping up to see what the excitement was. Harold glanced at him—and an odd expression passed over his face. His hands bobbed at his side, and then, as if suddenly afraid, he twisted the key in the ignition. The car jerked back and I heard my dog give a yelp and then a series of cries, like an echo traveling through space.

TWO

After the bus left us off, I started the mile-and-a-half walk home. The bus used to let us off on the corner of our street, Forest View Drive, but then last year not enough people voted for something called a bond issue, which would have raised more funds for our school system, but also would have raised taxes. So, along with crowded classrooms and worn-out textbooks, there were fewer buses. My mother said there weren't enough people with kids, that was why the vote had failed, but I wasn't sure that was it. It seemed like everybody had kids.

Keith, Jim, and Robby were walking ahead of me, along Wagoner Road. Usually they took the activity bus home from the sports they played, later in the afternoon. But it was after basketball season, and track was also one of the things that had been cut, so they were taking the regular bus. Behind me were a couple of girls from down the block. Way ahead of us all was Harold, who had sat as he always did in the single seat across the aisle from the bus driver, and who was now walking quickly, his arms pumping.

Jim stopped, and then Keith and Robby. They looked over at a lot where a house was being built: a skeleton of wooden planks, with sections of black tar-papered walls. There were upended wheelbarrows and piles of dirt in the yard, and a red line looped around stakes, marking off an area for the driveway. Inside, on the rough wooden floor, was a stack of bricks. Keith looked up and down the street; then he picked up a rock and flung it at one of the tar-papered walls. It hit with a dull thud, and I thought it must have made an indentation that would always be there, like a tooth mark in a fossil. I started walking more slowly. Since they were in eighth grade and I was in sixth, they could give me a hard time, grab my book bag or my cap, and I didn't feel like being messed around with. Robby picked up a piece of gravel and flung it at the house; it fell short, and landed on a pile of dirt.

"No way," said Keith, and Robby shrugged. Robby was shorter than the other two: they played first-string junior varsity; he played second.

I decided to walk past them, as they seemed intent on the house. Jim flicked back a long front strand of his hair and then stooped on the ground. Where the other two had just grabbed theirs, Jim was taking his time to find the right stone. He smiled a little to himself when he did, and then stood up and stared at the house.

The front door in the little square house to the left opened and an old man stuck his head out.

"That's enough, you boys," the man said. His eyes

were squinting, almost like he was a prisoner in that house and it was a shock to see the light of day.

I stopped where I was, as if I was one of those he was yelling at.

Jim stood there, still staring at the house, tossing and catching the stone. Jim was a good-looking guy, with brown hair that he wore long but combed so you couldn't really tell. He was maybe older than most eighth-graders, and was friends both with the rough kids who wanted to race cars and with the athletes, who respected his quickness and strength. There was a small legend at school about his winning a conference football game last fall with a 73-yard run, and it was pretty well known that he'd once shot a lit arrow into the door of an abandoned barn, off one of the back roads by school. Perhaps he'd just wanted to see it burning in the door, like in some kind of adventure, but the dried wood had caught and the barn had gone right up.

Jim tossed that stone up and down in his hand as if it was all his choice now, he could throw it, or not, or even decide to fling it through the man's front window, and he was keeping it long enough for the man to know that.

"Come on," said Keith. He'd been football captain and the pitcher for the baseball team. You'd always see him in his front driveway, playing catch with his father. I imagined he didn't want to go too far out of line.

Still, Jim flipped and caught the stone. Both Keith and the man were staring at him now. Finally the man cursed and closed his door, and Jim dropped the rock in a puddle.

I lifted my books a little higher under my arm and started walking. Then Keith said, "Hey, Donald."

"Yeah?" I said, and turned around. The sun was behind them and now I was the one who was squinting.

"So how you doing?"

"Good," I said. I looked at their faces, but I couldn't tell what they wanted.

"Well, that's great," he said.

Robby nodded.

"You know," said Keith, "I was sorry to hear about your dog." Behind him, Robby took a couple of steps like he had a limp. "Knock it off," said Keith. I pretended I hadn't seen it, and Jim didn't let on that he'd noticed it, either.

"So he's gonna be okay?"

I nodded.

"Well, that's great," said Robby.

"Cause I always liked that dog," said Keith. He walked toward me. "I remember that time when you first had him and he got loose. We were having dinner and my dad said, 'What the hell was that?' and we went to our window and there was this crazy Dalmatian charging through our trees. He could move!"

"Like a rabbit," said Robby.

"He always wanted the squirrels," I said, "but we had to keep him tied up. Even so, he almost caught one, and we had to shorten the lead." I was smiling, and then my throat got full.

Keith and Robby glanced at each other.

"That was pretty good shooting at that house," I

said. "I thought you were gonna hit that old guy, too."

Jim looked over at me and smiled a little. "I wouldn't do something like that," he said. It was the first thing he'd ever said to me.

We started walking up the road, the four of us. I was almost as tall as Robby, but with the other two I only came up past the shoulders of their jackets.

"Listen," said Keith. "We've been talking. It doesn't seem right what happened to your dog."

"Nobody having to pay," said Robby.

"His father came over with a check," I said.

"A *check*," said Keith. "And your mom and dad didn't take the money, right?"

"Well, no."

"Yeah! My parents wouldn't, either." Keith had a round face and short hair and a smile that he could turn on to teachers that made him look like the all-American kid. But I'd also seen his face turn red and his mouth tighten into a pout when he misthrew a pass or a pitch. He spoke more softly: "And even if they had taken it, so what? That would be between them. What about Harold?"

"What about you and Harold?" said Robby.

"It's like what he did to your dog sums up his life. Weird and lame."

"I don't know," I said.

"Why don't you cut off his foot?" said Robby, and laughed.

"I'm not saying anything like that," said Keith, and he smiled at me. "I'm just saying—well, what I said. It doesn't seem right. Nobody even bloody likes him."

14

"He's got those little round black glasses," said Robby.

"And his hair—God, he looks bald," said Keith.

"Like a Martian," said Robby, and I laughed, and Keith joined in.

"He must learn the laws of planet Earth!" said Keith in a strange voice, and we cracked up again, and then Jim looked at us and I stopped laughing. He'd grown suddenly serious, almost as if he knew—before any of us—what was to come.

"Yeah, like the law of gravity," said Robby, and held out one of his books and dropped it, and I laughed again, as if it were all just a goof.

Then we were at my street and we stopped. I glanced down it: Harold had vanished into his house.

"We're going over to Robby's," said Keith. Robby lived on a side street farther down; Keith lived another half mile down Wagoner, and Jim lived almost at its end in a small house. "But, you know, we always end up at the shack. You can usually find us there. And besides, we probably shouldn't talk in the open again."

"He probably doesn't know where the shack is," said Robby.

"I could find it," I said.

"Well, think it over," said Keith. He looked up and down the street. "You know, about what we talked about. About teaching him a lesson. Then give us the rebel yell."

"I don't think he'd know—"

"He'd know," Jim interrupted, and nodded at me. The rebel yell was a high-pitched cry. I'd heard it, when I was sitting on my front porch, heard it echoing out from the woods behind the houses across from us, back on the other side of the ravine, where the shack was.

"Okay," I said. "And thanks." I turned and started home. I didn't look back because I didn't want to see if Robby was limping again, to find out if it was all just a joke to them, or that maybe they knew a little how I felt.

It was still light when my father got home that evening. I was sitting out back with my dog. His head was down on his front paws, and his eyes had red lines in the white parts. His nose was dry. His rear foot was in a splint, and the paw that the Buick's tire had crushed was in plaster and gauze, wound around and around, so it looked like a beehive. I was petting him, and he'd close his eyes every time my hand came forward to start another stroke.

I heard a car door slam from the front of the house, and my father came around to the back door.

"Hey, Dad!" I yelled.

He stopped and looked at me and Chief. Then he nodded and went up the stairs. After a moment I turned back: Chief had lifted his head and was staring at where my father had been, as if waiting for him to come back.

Suddenly my eyes stung. "That little creep," I said. "That Harold, he'll pay." Chief dropped his head down. I knew I couldn't make him feel better, but I thought there might be some secret among packs of dogs or wolves that vowing revenge could help take away the pain. Chief closed his eyes. "I know, you just want to sleep," I said. "But don't worry, boy."

My mother and father were sitting in the living room when I came in. On the coffee table in front of him, my father had a can of beer and shot of whiskey. My mother had a tall glass of ginger ale. It didn't seem as if they'd been talking.

"How's Chief?" my mother asked brightly.

"He looks like he's been run over by a car," I said.

Her eyes clouded over.

"He needs to come in," I said. "He probably gets cold. And the stupid squirrels . . ." My father was looking down at his beer can. He still had his work clothes on: a white shirt, with a plastic penholder in his pocket that said RANDALL FOODS. He had been a stock clerk there, before the war. After he came back, he found they hadn't held the job for him. But then there had been an opening about the time I was born, and now he was the grocery manager.

"You know he can't come in the house," said my mother, glancing at my father to make sure it was still so.

"I know, he was making all kinds of noise," I said. "But now he's quiet. He's sick. From that stupid Harold. It doesn't seem right, him not having to— I don't know why he was sitting in that car anyway."

"It was an accident," said my mother. "Some things can't be helped."

My father took a sip of beer and put the can down, and there was a little curl of foam still on his upper lip. "It is hard to see him that way," he said quietly.

"But he's still there," I said to my mother. "He's still

17

out there. He'll always be out there." My eyes were stinging again.

My father took a cigarette from the pack he kept behind the holder in his shirt pocket, and started tapping it on the table.

"He will be okay," said my mother. "The vet said so. He'll just have a limp. Like that character, on that Western show."

"*Gunsmoke*," I said. "That stupid Chester."

"Yes," said my mother, "like Chester."

I went to my room, but I didn't go in right away. I stood there looking at my unmade bed, my schoolbooks and baseball glove, the globe of the world, and the coins I hadn't yet gone through on my desk. I don't think they'd even wanted a dog, but I'd made such a fuss over getting one. And now I'd said some things I probably shouldn't have.

I sat on my bed, and then at my desk, but I couldn't work on the coins. All I had to do was lift my head a little and I'd be able to see the Buick in Harold's driveway, parked there as if nothing had happened.

My mother had finished those curtains. I pulled them shut—and then I just saw sailboats, heading out, on a wide, wide sea.

THREE

I traced a line between the houses facing ours; I angled off through low trees and weeds that ended in the ravine, where I scrambled down, as loose rocks and dirt rained on either side. I hopped from one stone to another across the creek, and ran up the other side of the gully, feeling like I might fall backward until I reached level ground, where the trees grew high and dense. I had to wander around a little, until the shack came into view.

Robby had been wrong; I could find the way there.

I looked back in the direction I'd come and then I took a couple steps toward the shack. It was made of plywood and cardboard, with some black boards they probably stole from a construction site. The roof was a rusted square of tin. I stood outside it for a while, with the wind blowing through the tops of the tall trees. Then I cupped my hands around my mouth and gave a kind of high yell that came out higher than I'd wanted. It couldn't hurt to hear what their idea was.

I waited there, and finally the shack door—painted red, with a crack down its center where pale wood showed—opened, and Robby stuck his head out.

"You were right," he said to someone inside. "He showed up."

Keith was leaning against a small, wobbly table. Pulled up to it was a crate standing on its side, and a spindly kitchen chair. Jim was sitting on a ripped-up bucket seat from a car, facing slightly away from where the other two must have been sitting before I came in.

"So," said Keith. He smiled and extended his hand for me to sit, the way people did on TV when they were showing someone into their offices to do something like blackmail. I chose the chair; I thought the crate might be too high, that my feet wouldn't reach the floor.

Nobody said anything for a while. I still wasn't sure they really wanted me here; I knew the thing for me to do, the most essential thing, was to keep quiet and not act like I was really interested or even wanted to be there. On the wall to my right was a calendar with a white 1958 Chevy Impala, and on the wall next to it another one with a photo of a blonde practically coming out of her yellow swimsuit.

"He's checkin' her out," said Robby.

I looked away, but I knew my face was red.

"It's okay," said Keith. "It means you're normal."

"Probably Harold wouldn't even look," I said, and Keith and Robby laughed. Jim just sat there, flipping a stick back and forth, hitting the side of the seat and then his knee.

"Old Harold," said Robby. "Oh, why doesn't he just give him a bloody nose," he said suddenly to Keith.

"That's too simple," said Keith, as if explaining something to a child. "We don't know if a bloody bloody nose would make any difference to him."

"He'd feel it," said Robby, and punched the black part of the wall where he was standing, leaving a small dent with his knuckles. The tar-papered board seemed to have shifted slightly from where it had been nailed. "Donald could just knock his books out of his hand, and when Harold asked why, he could deck him."

"Big deal," said Keith.

"I thought that's what you guys wanted."

Keith sat down on the crate. "That would be over in a few seconds. And Donald"—he nodded toward me—"Donald might get in some kind of trouble." He paused. "I had in mind something that would last longer."

"Like as long as track season would have lasted," said Jim.

"Well, it's bloody better than anything you've come up with—better than hanging out here smoking Marlboros."

"Would you stop saying 'bloody.' "

"I'll bloody well say it if I want to."

Jim shifted the seat around so he was facing toward Keith. "Just don't overuse it," he said. Then he started flipping the stick again.

Keith shook his head slightly, and let out a breath.

"I still don't get it," said Robby.

"That's cause you're a fool," said Keith. "It's just time we do something big. Something that everyone will remember." He stared at me. "And, Donald, you

21

could be part of it. Harold's had it coming, even before that thing with your dog."

"Anyone can see that," said Robby.

"We want to try a kind of experiment," said Keith. "If you do want to get him back, this is the way. Who knows? Maybe it won't work. It'll be fun, anyway. And if it does work—"

"It'll be like the arrow!" said Robby, as if he suddenly understood. "Everybody still talks about that!"

Keith glanced over at Jim, and Jim met Keith's eye, before he went back to his work with the stick.

"You know, you shouldn't ever talk to us about that," Keith said to Robby, but he was looking at me. I acted like it was no big deal if both of them had been in on it. "But, yeah, you're right," Keith continued. "It'll be like the . . . bloody burning arrow. Only better. It'll be even more planned out. Like some illegal psychology project or something." He put his hands in front of him on the table and folded them together. "You'll have to find out all about him, Donald. And the first thing is"—here he smiled a little—"you're going to be his friend."

FOUR

arold had moved in al-
most two years ago, when his father was transferred to
the new Chevy–Buick dealership on the main com-
mercial strip in town. He had started class one morning at the end of that year, during fourth grade, with
only about six weeks of school left. It was so weird to
have a new kid come in at that time—the middle of
spring—that when he'd been brought in, the other
kids had stopped hanging up their coats and putting
their books in their desks and just crowded around
and stared at him, until the teacher broke it up. I'd
heard this from someone who was there when it happened.

The day after I visited the shack, I asked Kevin,
David, and Rich if they knew much about him. I asked
it in a kind of casual way, as we were getting our trays
for lunch. Kevin shook his head. Rich thought he did
but then decided it was someone else he was thinking
of, a big kid named Harvey. David said he did—he

had been in Harold's class the year after he'd first started at our school.

"But he got transferred out—right in September—into Mrs. Griffon's." Mrs. Griffon was an elderly teacher who had a small class of advanced students. "Why do you care about *him?*" he asked, turning toward me.

I shrugged. "He lives on my block." I hadn't told anyone the whole story about Chief, and definitely not about Jim and Keith and Robby.

David grabbed a plate covered with roast beef and mashed potatoes and drowned in brown gravy that had a skin on it.

"I probably never said four words to him," he went on. "He's supposed to be a whiz in math. In Griffon's they didn't even know what to do with him. They tried him in some seventh- or eighth-grade class, but it didn't work. The older kids kept getting pissed off at him. I don't think he's in a regular sixth-grade class now. Mrs. Saunders just works with him on her own. I remember"—he laughed—"he had this lunch box with rockets and stars on it—it seemed like it should belong to some little first-grader. Somebody teased him about it, and then he never brought the lunch box again."

"I wonder why he had a lunch box like that," I said.

"To bring his *lunch* in, I guess!" David leaned out of the line until he spotted Rich, who was a couple of kids behind us. All over the room there were trays clattering, and kids yelling back and forth, and wadded-up napkins and wax paper being tossed. The neighborhood lady who worked as the lunch monitor was

24

trying not to notice, as if she'd walked in on a strange tribe and thought it safer not to comment on their customs.

"Hey, Rich, Donald's getting weird."

"I always knew he had it in him," said Rich, and he and Kevin snickered.

"It's because they're making me eat this," I said, pointing to the food on the tray, and they all cracked up.

That afternoon, on the bus ride home, I thought things over. And when the bus stopped, I got off as quickly as I could, and caught up with Harold right where the new house was being built on Wagoner Road. You could see progress: wooden siding over the black tar paper, a frame where the front door would be. I wondered who might move in there, if they would have a kid my age.

Harold was walking in his concentrated way, books under his right arm, left arm swinging stiffly. He didn't slacken his pace as I came up alongside, and I walked with him a moment, turning over what I was going to say to him in my mind. Keith was right. His hair *was* so short that he looked bald, and his skin was completely pale.

"I was wondering . . ." I said.

Arms swinging, head downward, as if he hadn't heard me.

"I mean, I had a question for you."

We walked a few more paces.

"It's about math," I said, and now he stopped and glared at me through his glasses. He was just a slight kid, but I felt on the spot. Then I plunged ahead. "I've got this math problem," I said. "It's giving me trouble. And someone, someone said you were good in math, so I wondered. Wondered if you had any ideas."

He was gazing down at the road, and I had no idea what he was thinking of what I said.

"It's one of those story problems," I continued. "A tricky one, about test pilots and airplanes." I had rehearsed this well. "There are four guys and they're supposed to each work one shift per week, but there are seven jets. And then one of the guys gets sick."

"He gets sick?" asked Harold.

"Yeah," I said. "Maybe he gets altitude sickness or something." I laughed a little, but his mouth stayed in a thin line.

"Let me see it," he said.

"Great," I said, and started to take a few steps. It seemed so easy suddenly, we were to be going to his house . . . But he wasn't moving, so I stopped, too.

"Here?" I said. I took a breath and walked back. Jim, Keith, and Robby were walking some ways behind us. Jim was staring at the house that was being built and Robby was bobbing his head like a fighter. But Keith had stopped. He was just watching.

I took the math book out and opened it to the page I'd marked with a piece of notebook paper. The girls from down the block passed by, and I hoped they couldn't tell that I was asking for his help. Harold took a pencil from his pocket, and jotted down a few fractions on the notebook paper. I could tell he'd hardly bothered to read it, but had figured most of it out in his head from what I had said. Then he wrote "QED."

"What's that?" I said.

He pushed his glasses back on his nose. " *'Quod erat demonstrandum.'* Latin. It means, 'Which was to be demonstrated.' "

"Uh-huh."

As I put the math book back, he brought out from his pocket a folded-over brown paper bag he must have had his lunch in. He opened it and took out a cookie. It was homemade, and seemed a little too well done. As if he'd forgotten I was there, he broke off a piece and put it in his mouth. Then he started walking, arms pumping, chewing now.

I walked with him. "Cookie *erat* gobbled," I said.

"What?"

"Forget it," I said. Now I just wanted to forget the whole plan. He almost gave me a creepy feeling, and I didn't like the way he had put me on the spot. I thought about Robby's idea, of just hitting him in the nose, but I'd never been in a fight.

I kept pace with him a little while longer. Then I felt myself slowing down as he walked ahead, until both of us were on our own again.

In my room that afternoon, sitting at my desk, going through some pennies I was sure I'd already examined, I tried to think what else I had found out that I could tell them. None of it seemed any good. When Richard Kenny, the paper boy, had asked me how my dog was, I'd said fine, and then asked him if he'd ever seen Harold do anything else strange like lock himself in the car. He said no, they were just regular customers. They took the daily paper, as well as the

Sunday edition. And one Saturday a month or so Harold and his family were gone somewhere in their Buick, and he couldn't collect that day, but had to wait till the next Saturday. But they always paid what they were supposed to.

I didn't see how any of that was much help.

The only things my mother had to offer was that they had had their driveway resurfaced last autumn, and that Harold's parents seemed to keep to themselves. She also remembered seeing his father early one Sunday morning, putting golf clubs in the car trunk. And she once saw Harold's mother talking with Mrs. Griffon at a parent-teacher night. "The funny thing about it—oh, I suppose it isn't funny . . ."

"What," I said. "What funny thing?"

"Mrs. Griffon was gesturing and smiling in that way she does when she raves about a student, and Harold's mother . . ." My mother shrugged.

"*What?*"

"She was wearing that scarf she wears sometimes, and she was chewing gum. But not just, not just regular gum. Every now and then a little pink bubble would come out of her mouth, and she'd snap it."

"That's it?" I said. "She was chewing gum?"

"Why are you so interested in Harold?"

"You know something, I'm not," I said, and I suddenly felt I was telling the truth. None of this was working, nothing I had found out added up to anything: his father golfed, his mother chewed gum, they paid their bills on time, Harold was a whiz in math. And I didn't know what any of it would matter, anyhow, even if I did find out something. I had no idea what Keith meant, "some illegal psychology project,"

28

and I didn't want to ask, I didn't want to look as stupid as Robby, I just wanted to find out something about Harold that would make what the plan was become suddenly clear. If his father was a Russian spy, if he had the plans for Fort Knox in his golf bag—then, bingo, we could turn him into the FBI. But all I had was that their driveway was in good shape for the winter.

That evening, when Chief saw me come out of the back door, he ran to the end of his chain, holding his rear foot in the air. Perhaps one too many squirrels had made fun of him for being laid up, so he'd gotten back some of his speed.

"Cut it out, Chief!"

He was pushing against me with his nose, and half jumping on me to get to the food bowl I was carrying. Lately there were sometimes bits of hamburger meat mixed up in his usual dog food—one night there had been fat from lamb chops.

"Mind your bloody manners," I said. That was something I had found out, when I sat behind Robby on the bus on a day that Keith and Jim were staying after school. Robby was explaining to another eighth-grader how Keith had found out that "bloody" was a swear word in England that was more offensive than most run-of-the-mill swear words if you knew what it meant.

But it didn't seem to affect Chief, who was sniffing madly at the bowl as I put it down. I dropped it by his house and stepped back and watched him nose around the maroon clumps of dog food.

I looked away, down through the back yards, a

whole row of them with trees and shrubs, none of them as well maintained as ours. But they all had their own little communities of squirrels and birds taunting the pets who strained to get at them, spaniels barking wildly and getting the house windows smeared with their noses when they saw a squirrel; toms jumping against the pane as a bird fluttered away. Sometimes you could find the carcass of a chipmunk or field mouse that had pushed his luck when a dog or cat was out of the house.

I heard the back door close. My father was coming out, with a plate of something in his hand. Chief turned away from the half-eaten food and sat at attention, his tail switching, looking for a moment like a real firehouse dog, hearing the alarm go off.

Sometimes when my father hadn't shaved for a day he had what he called a five-o'clock shadow—the outline of a beard that wasn't really there. Now he had a kind of five-o'clock shadow of a smile on his face. He was carrying a white paper plate with a hamburger on it—the paper was blotched with grease. Chief watched him as he brought it down to his bowl—he didn't nose him like he had me. After my father dropped the burger into the bowl and stood up, Chief tore off a piece, then lifted his head and snapped it down.

"Good boy," said my father. He picked up a couple of sticks while Chief chewed. When the last patches of snow melted, he'd make sure he gathered them all, so they wouldn't mar the carpet of grass he'd gotten to grow even under the trees. When people complimented him for keeping the yard so nicely maintained—there were lines of trimmed shrubs, and patches of flowers, and a special kind of Kentucky grass in front—he always said it was just a way to keep his mind busy.

"Yard looks good," said my father, nodding, still with that smile.

"It sure does," I said. Chief was staring up at us, and his eyes were bright. This now seemed enough for me: being with my dad and my dog in our yard, the sun's rays slanting through the trees. Chief was getting better, and whatever it was that Keith had in mind wasn't as important as this.

Chief had finished his hamburger, and I smiled up at my father, but something changed on his face. I turned to the dog, and saw he was hobbling away, taking uneven steps back toward his house. My father was looking away, into the other yards.

It seemed to me then that everything changed, or perhaps changed back to what it had been. There really was something wrong with our dog, something that would never go away.

"Sit down, you bloody dog," I yelled.

Chief looked at me, not understanding.

"I wouldn't use that word," said my father. He was still staring into the back yards. I'd forgotten he'd known some English guys in the war.

"I'm sorry," I said. I'm sorry, I said to Chief without speaking it. I thought of the cool way Jim flipped the stick back and forth, of Robby hitting the wall, of what Keith had said. They wouldn't let anyone do this to them. If they really wanted to, they'd find out what the plan was, and they'd figure out a way to get back.

"I better go get my smokes," said my father.

31

"Sure," I said, but it was me who was leaving. I'd broken away from something and was already scrambling up the ravine, seeing the tar-paper walls through the trees.

FIVE

We need more than that he's good in math," said Keith.

"Keith already knows it," said Robby. "He was in his class for a couple of weeks."

"I know, it's hardly anything. But what I don't know is, how this all would work. A psychology project, an illegal psychology project . . . It's like if you send someone on some mission, and you say, go up, go up to the top of that hill—" Keith and Robby were sitting on the other sides of the table, and Jim was, as before, tipping back on the car seat on the floor. "But you don't tell them there's a town there, you don't tell them there's some village named Baden Schweinstein or something and what they have to watch out for and what they're supposed to do to the town, how exactly they're supposed to blow it up or something, or . . ." I took a breath. "So I don't know what the whole thing is, the whole deal why you want to find this stuff about him out for, if you tell me that, well, then . . ."

Nobody said anything for a moment. Then Keith laughed and said, "Hey, take it easy . . ."

I nodded and tried to laugh with him.

"You are kind of right, in a way," Keith said. "It is kind of like a campaign." He motioned to Jim.

"Go ahead and tell them," Jim said. "I don't care." I guessed Robby hadn't heard the story, either.

Keith wove his fingers together and straightened out his arms, as if he were getting ready to grab a bat and his father was watching.

"There was this bloody guy that liked Jim's mother—"

"Leave that part out," said Jim. The seat was flat on the floor now and he was sitting straight up in it. I knew that his parents were divorced, that his father lived in Akron.

"So there was this bloody guy," said Keith. "A stupid big fat guy—with bad eyes. Wouldn't you say, Jim?"

Jim was leaning back again, chewing on a long piece of grass.

"Anyway, he worked in the park," continued Keith. "Let's say his name was Randy McGee."

"The names are being changed to protect the innocent," said Robby, laughing, and then stopped suddenly when the other two didn't respond.

"Randy McGee did all kinds of things in the park. He did some cement work on the walks, and he transported the picnic tables when they needed repairing. And sometimes he drove the honeydipper."

"The honeydipper?" I asked.

"It's what they call the truck with the long rubber tube and the tank that cleans out the outhouses," said

Keith with a smirk. "Now, Randy McGee had a son, let's call him Tommy, who sometimes helped out in the park." Robby started to laugh again, but bit his lip to stop himself. "And Randy and his son, Tommy, were spending time around a certain person's house, on account of—well, they just were. And the boy who lived in that house—let's call him Robin Hood."

"For shooting arrows!" said Robby, and he did laugh this time, and so did I.

"Just tell the story," Jim said. There was a vein in his forehead I hadn't noticed before.

"Now Robin Hood didn't like Randy and his son, Tommy. It was sort of an insult having a man who drove a honeydipper sitting on your couch, making small talk with your mom. And his son sitting next to him, drinking your pop, and watching midget-car racing on your bloody TV."

Jim had bitten off an end of the weed, and was chewing on it, and taking bits of it out of his mouth with his fingers.

"So how do you get rid of such a thing—growing in your house like mold?"

"Beat him up?" said Robby.

Keith shook his head. "Your problem, Robby my boy, is you've got to be trickier. If you beat him up, you get in trouble. And his old man tells your mom. No, you have to get him to *want* to not be there." Keith nodded to himself, as if satisfied with his explanation. "I'll give you a clue. Robin was able to talk to his Merry Men all, and some of them knew people who worked in the park where Randy and Tommy worked."

"Riding the honeydipper!" said Robby.

"Whatever he bloody did," snapped Keith, and he seemed really angry for a moment.

"So what'd you do?" Robby asked, turning to Jim, who ignored him.

"What would you do?" Keith asked Robby and me.

"Flatten the old man's tires," said Robby.

"If you knew people who knew him," I said slowly, "then maybe you could find out something. Some way to—I don't know—"

Jim was looking at me.

"That's right," said Keith. "So what do you imagine we found out about them?"

Robby and I both shook our heads.

"By the sewage plant, a couple of years before, Tommy was walking around in the grass. He stepped in a nest of snakes. Those suckers went slithering every which way, but at least one of them took off after him, over the gravel where the honeydipper was parked. They said it looked like somebody being chased by a W."

Keith laid his hands one on top of the other on the table. "Whether Tommy'd ever been afraid of snakes before, he sure was after that. Every time they went back there, he was half out of his mind. He wouldn't get out of the truck, and even the tube on the truck scared him sometimes if he saw it out of the corner of his eye. His father, old Randy, thought it was a riot. He used to laugh about it with the guys—you know those guys, in their green work clothes with their beer bellies hanging over their belts."

"But then he didn't think it was so funny," said Jim.

Keith waited to see if Jim would go on, and then he

continued. "He didn't think it was so funny when his son would get out of his car at a certain person's house and see a flicker in the grass. 'Didja see that?' he'd say to his father, and his father would push his thick bloody pop-bottle glasses against the top of his nose and squint. But by then Tommy would be back in the car. With the doors locked. Or maybe he'd make a dash for the house."

Keith rubbed his round chin with his hands, and then looked from Robby to me. "And finally there was the time he went into the house and when he came back out to wait for his father—after he'd drunk all the orange soda he'd wanted—and then in that car he heard a thump, like a dog's tail, from the back seat. But the people he was visiting didn't have a dog." Keith suppressed a smile.

"They must have left the car window open . . ." said Jim.

"For a blacksnake to get inside," said Keith, and they both grinned.

"Of course, old Tommy stopped coming around," said Keith.

"And his father?" I asked.

Jim glanced at me, and there was a hint of a smile. "I guess she got sick of him," he said.

"Jesus, how did you train the snakes?" asked Robby.

Keith laughed. "There was only one snake—the blacksnake at the end. Other than that, it was just a belt tugged with fishing line."

I realized I'd been leaning forward, and now I sat back. Jim stood up and stretched, and I tried to imagine him lying in the grass, or around the corner of the garage, patiently tugging on the line, being careful not to laugh or make any noise, intent on what he was doing, as if the world rested on it. It was not a way I had ever thought of him before.

Keith turned to me. "I think you get the idea," said Keith. "If you really want to pay him back, we need to find out the thing that's Harold's snake."

It was almost dinnertime when I left the shack, but rather than go straight home, I crossed the ravine and headed right. I stayed behind the houses that were across from mine, and went down about four, until I was behind Harold's house. No leaves were out yet, so I had a pretty clear view of the back of it. There was the same green siding as in the front; the lawn here seemed rougher, with clumps of crabgrass showing from beneath the last patches of snow. I didn't know what I expected to find, but I knew I had to be more concentrated in my search. When my legs hurt from kneeling, I sat on the ground, even though I had gone right to the shack from the bus and was still wearing my school clothes.

I tried not to get discouraged as I didn't see anything; I thought how Jim had had to find out things and set the stage before he could finally make his move.

And then I did spot something. The Buick was gone, so I knew his father hadn't gotten back from work yet. I figured his mother was somewhere in the house, maybe on the phone, or watching TV and chewing gum. But as I stared at the back of the house I could see someone. Harold. The round shape of his head seemed to come into focus in the only dark back window of the house—the way the moon shows up as the sky around it gets dark. I wasn't sure if he'd been there all along, or if he'd just come. I knew that I'd been careful not to show myself, even when I hadn't seen anyone at first. But the way he was staring out, it was as if he'd spotted me and was waiting for me to walk out of the woods and through his back yard, bringing whatever it was I was going to bring.

SIX

1 tried to keep a close eye on him, and ask around whenever there was the chance. I had an idea that if I could only find out why he'd locked himself in the car that day, I might have something we could use. Other than what Richard Kenny had said, about him and his family being off on a driving trip every three or four weeks, the subject of the car never came up.

A girl I knew had been in Mrs. Griffon's class with Harold that first year: for his science project he had brought in a collection of insects. Maybe he was really into bugs; it would fit, science and his interest in math. According to our encyclopedia, the study of insects was called entomology. I wondered how I could bring that into a conversation with him, someday after school when I caught up with him as he bolted from the bus. If I could find out for sure that he had a collection, maybe we could let them out all over his house. I imagined beetles in his oatmeal, and moths

with see-through wings in his parents' coffee at breakfast, a whole alien invasion of freed bugs. But then I
realized if he was a collector the insects were already
dead.

At night, I'd sit on my desk and watch his house
from my bedroom window. I was pretty sure his room
was the one with the single window, on the side of the
house facing me.

And it seemed to fit. He was a weird kid, and his
bedroom was lit at weird times. Sometimes, after the
rest of the house was dark, his light would come on,
and stay on for a while. Other times, it would still be
early, the living-room light would be on, and his light
would be off. Maybe he was just watching TV with his
parents, but for some reason I didn't think so. I imagined him there in his room, with his light on, and then
off, and if that was so, he must be doing something. In
the light and in the dark. Dissecting fireflies? Figuring
out math problems by flashlight? What would someone do in the dark?

Some days I did try to catch up with him after
school. Once or twice I said something about how
helpful he had been with the math, and that my
teacher had been impressed with the "QED" I'd put at
the end of the problems I'd solved.

"Except when I get them wrong," I said, and
laughed, but he just kept walking straight ahead.

I once again had the feeling that, as much as I might
want it to, our plan against him would never work.
Unless I tried something different.

The first weekend in March it was suddenly warm.

I walked without a jacket through the yards of the houses across the street, and then into the woods. There were a few birds hopping around under the trees, fluttering in the deadwood and pools of water. I cut left and walked through the thin trees and brush until I was behind Harold's house.

He and his father were in the back yard, and I felt my heart pounding. I made myself calm down and watch. His father was swinging a golf club and whacking these little plastic balls way out to the end of their lot. Then it was Harold's turn. He had a shorter metal club that didn't seem like the right kind. He walked up and took a swing with the club, and even from where I was, I could see it was all wrong the way he did it. It was like he was gripping a bat and trying to hit a baseball at his feet. It was the way a little kid would do it. He swung wildly and missed each time; then he dropped the club on the ground. His father came up and hit the balls, and then it was Harold's turn again, and this time he swung even more wildly. As he was setting up to try again—he must have nicked the ball because it dribbled away from him a couple of inches—I saw his father turn and look into the back window of their house. He faced that way awhile, as Harold swung, and when he looked back at his son he had a funny grin on his face. Poor guy must be embarrassed.

After Harold swung at another ball, his father took his club and made another couple of swings. He may have been showing him how to do it, but he swung pretty hard, as if he was just trying to knock that ball as far as he could. I figured they were going to keep on doing this, so I took a few steps out of the trees, just as a little red plastic ball went humming past my head.

His father stopped swinging when he saw me, and waved. Harold just stared at me, through those little glasses, and I thought maybe we didn't have to do anything at all to him, just let him live his life and he'd be miserable enough.

"Are you much for golf?" asked his father as I came near. His father didn't seem like a bad guy. He had a young look about him, blond hair and smooth skin on his cheeks. He seemed easygoing when he was smiling. When he was serious, when he was lining up a shot, he looked as if something had just gone wrong. He had thin arms and a small potbelly.

I shrugged my shoulders.

"Harold and I wouldn't mind a threesome. Would we, Harold?" Harold glared, and his father's smile disappeared for a second. Then it came right back. "What say we let Donald give it a try?"

Harold just stood there. His father walked over and took the short club out of his hand. He handed it to me; then he put a little bright yellow plastic ball on the ground and stood over it as if he was going to hit it. "See how I hold my hands?" There was a smell of coffee on his breath.

He stepped away and I put my hands on the club and stood over the ball, and then I glanced up at him. He was looking back up at the window, as if someone was there; then he seemed to sense my pause and turned toward me, smiling in that funny way again.

"That's the boy," he said.

I heard one of Harold's shoes tapping against the

other as he watched. I took my hands back for the swing—Harold might feel bad for a little while if I did it right, but that wouldn't be enough, and his father would keep taking him out and showing him until he got it—so I switched my grip on the upswing, and when I brought the club down against the ball I had my hands in Harold's awkward batter's grip. The head of my club bounced against the ground and spit out a big chunk of dirt. The ball remained where it was.

"See, he can't do it, either," said Harold. There was a sarcastic tone in his voice. I didn't know why he was being such a jerk to his father.

"That's called a 'divot,' " said his father.

"Oh, who cares," said Harold, and turned and walked off. His father watched him go and then turned to me. But it wasn't him I was paying attention to now. I could see Harold's mother behind him in the window; her eyes appeared stricken and she had her hand half over her mouth, as if she was trying not to cry.

When I came around the side of the house, I saw Harold sitting on the front porch. He had taken out a crumpled paper bag from his pants pocket, and was eating a cookie.

"What do you want?" he asked as I approached.

"I just can't take too much of that stuff," I said.

"Which *stuff?*" The way his mouth was moving and how his eyes looked small from his glasses made me think of a rabbit.

"Sports stuff," I said. I sat down next to him, and

stared out, as he was staring. Down the street, I could see my house: ranch-style, brick in front, shrubs down the sides of the driveway in perfect rows, like a yard in a magazine.

"I saw you playing baseball," he said. It sounded like he was accusing me of something. "I saw you get a hit."

"When?"

"Last year—in that lot." That would have been the lot on Wagoner, where we used to play before they started building the house.

"Just cause I can do it doesn't mean I like it," I said.

He thought about that for a moment, and then he made the slightest motion of his head—a nod. He finished the cookie and flicked the crumbs off his upper lip with his finger. "I don't know about you," he said, not meeting my eyes.

"What's there to know?"

"Why you're here." He seemed bothered—bugged. The word "entomology" flashed through my mind. "Because I do know," he said. "I do know. Your parents sent you over."

"My parents?" My mouth was dry.

"Of course," he said. "Because of . . . the . . ." I saw him mouth the word "dog" as if he couldn't get it out.

"No, no, it's nothing like that," I said. "Heck, my being here has nothing to do with my parents."

He was staring down at the sidewalk.

"The . . . dog's okay," I said. "He'll be fine. I mean, it's just a dog." He was watching an ant struggling with a brown crumb of the cookie. It was just a crumb, but to him it must have been a treasure.

"You know, this stuff doesn't matter," said Harold. He was quiet. "You don't know what I mean."

"I guess not." We both watched the ant.

"None of this matters. Baseball. Or golf. That doesn't matter, either."

"That's right," I said.

"I thought maybe you could see that," he said. "And that's why you messed up with the golf club—I know you can do better—but maybe you were showing me."

"Showing you?"

He glanced at me.

"Which was to be demonstrated," I said softly, and now he nodded.

"Exactly," he said. "That matters. Math. And other things. Others. People have no idea." He stood suddenly as if something had jerked him up. "I have to be getting in," he said. He leaned out and stared in the front window of his house. I didn't think he could see anything in the shaded glass.

"Maybe it's like the math," I said. I felt there was a door closing, and I had to prop it open somehow. "Maybe I'll need a little help before I get it."

He shot me a look; then he opened the screen door and slipped inside, while I stayed a little longer on his steps.

SEVEN

I walked home with him some days after school. He usually wouldn't say much, and I would make a few comments about something interesting I'd discovered doing my math homework, or how stupid sports were. He never mentioned the things he had said when we were sitting on his front porch; I was pretty sure he was waiting and watching, trying to figure out if he could trust me before he offered anything else.

He still hadn't mentioned anything about his bug collection. I hit on the idea of telling him about my coins as a way to lead into the subject. Not to say something stupid, like Lincoln looked like a grasshopper or something, but just enough to get him started.

It was a breezy day; Harold and I were walking quickly up the road from the bus. Jim, Keith, and Robby were nowhere to be seen, staying after school for some reason; either they were in trouble or were helping the baseball coach get ready for the coming season. As we neared our street, I mentioned that I was always looking through my mother's change for anything that was rare, and for one penny in particular.

"The 1909 S VDB," I said. "It was minted in San Francisco—that's why it has the S—in 1909, of course. The VDB stands for Victor D. Brenner, the guy who designed the Lincoln cent. His initials only appeared on the back of the coin in that year. There weren't many minted with both the S and the VDB." I paused. "If you find one it's worth a lot of money."

"How much?"

"I don't know. It depends on the condition. Maybe more than a hundred dollars."

"What would you do with it?" he asked.

"The money? I don't know. I never thought about it. I just know how great it would be to find it. I know it's out there—people are handing it to each other when they buy gum or cigarettes, but they don't bother to check."

I was talking too much about the coins.

"So," I said, "so I bet it's like that if you find a rare bug, too."

He didn't respond, he just kept walking, past the sentinels of mailboxes, the stones people put to mark the sides of their driveways. I could have been right on target or I could have been light-years away, and he could have thought I was just talking to myself. But I figured I must have hit on something. Right before we got to his house, he brought out a small brown paper bag and took a cookie out of it. Without saying anything, he broke off a small piece and handed it to me.

That Saturday, the Buick was gone. They must have left early in the morning, before I was up. They were probably on a family trip somewhere, driving out to buy maple syrup or visiting a zoo. But I hadn't seen them go, and I fell asleep that night before they returned. It probably had nothing to do with what I was looking for, but I decided I needed to be more watchful.

Three nights later, I was sitting on my desk, spying his house through my bedroom window. The lights were on in the living room and in his bedroom. And then it suddenly hit me, why they had been going off and on in his room: photography. It was so logical I felt stupid for not seeing it before. It must be dark in his room because he was using it for a *darkroom*. He must be developing pictures. A friend of my parents had shown us once how it was done: in this completely black room with a little red light he held a blank sheet of paper under some liquid in which he'd mixed chemicals, and then slowly lines had formed, and shading, until a clear picture—it was a photograph of a barn—appeared. Harold was developing pictures in his room! It would fit, chemicals with his interest in math. But what was he photographing? Insects? I had gotten somewhere, and then nowhere all at once. And even if he was developing pictures, what could we do with that?

I hadn't talked to Jim or Keith or Robby since they had told me about the trick with the snake. One day, I'd gone around to the shack, but there'd been no one there; I'd given the rebel yell and then finally pushed open the door hanging crooked on its hinges, and called their names. There wasn't any sign of them, but it looked like an animal had gotten in—a squirrel or maybe a raccoon: there were candy wrappers in little pieces scattered about. I left pretty quickly. I hadn't gone back there again, and even though I'd seen them at an assembly where some guy did magic tricks, I understood I shouldn't act like I knew them. It wouldn't be good if Harold saw. They were sitting and making jokes with some girl who had teased blond hair. I'd just gone and sat with the rest of my sixth-grade class. But all the time this guy made flowers come out of handkerchiefs and a real duck appear under a cake cover, I worried they weren't really interested anymore.

I focused again on Harold's house. His light was off. It had been on a minute before, hadn't it? But maybe I was getting one night of looking at Harold's house mixed up with another.

The light came on again for a moment. Then just as quickly clicked off. I slid from my desk. Maybe I was making the whole thing up, or maybe he was taking photographs of praying mantises, but either way I had to know. Even if we couldn't do anything with it.

I needed to take a closer look.

I opened my door quietly, so my mother wouldn't hear. My father was working late at the store and she was watching a news program in the living room and ironing—I could hear the sound of the iron shooting steam every couple of seconds. I went out the back door without making any noise.

Chief's chain rattled and he barked. Sometimes his bark was dry, like a cough. "It's me, boy," I said in a whisper from the back sidewalk. His chain clinked a few more times, and then he settled down.

It was cold tonight, and I shivered a little as I strode alongside our house, across the street, and between the houses there. Through her lit window I could see Mrs. Richard, the neighbor who lived opposite us, moving a checkered towel around the inside of a pan.

When I reached the edge of the woods behind her house, I cut left. Behind Harold's house I paused and caught my breath. There were all kinds of bug sounds in the woods behind me. Some of them had stopped when I'd arrived and now they were sawing away again, a whole world of entomology. I ran in a crouch toward his house. Halfway there I felt a pressure in the ball of my right foot, and saw I'd stepped on one of the golf balls his father had shot into the grass.

I went along the back of his house. If he or his parents happened to see me, it would be impossible to explain what I was doing there.

At the back left corner of the house I paused again. Then I started toward where I'd seen the light come and go in the window to his room.

I almost walked into it. Where I stopped all of a sudden, I could easily have reached out and touched the dark shape, but I knew I'd better not move, that he was just a couple of feet from me on the other side of the wall of his house. He'd not only shut off the light, he'd opened his window and must have unhooked his screen and now the end of the telescope was sticking out.

I could put my face in front of it and cross my eyes and show my teeth, and maybe he'd think a monster had come down and for a second he'd be scared out of his wits . . . It wasn't photography, or bugs. He was some kind of astronomy nut. It still wasn't much. But at least it explained why his room went dark when he was in it. I stood there, barely breathing, just outside the square of his window, and watched. The black round end of the tube moved just a little—I could see a glint in the lens—and then didn't move again.

I turned my head around and tried to figure out where he was gazing. There was some light from the moon scattered over the sky; I could see the Big Dipper, and a whole lot of other stars, some faint, some bright.

The telescope seemed to be pointed toward a section of sky where there were some pretty bright stars. He could be staring at those. I crouched down and put my back against his house, directly under the telescope. There was a group of several stars to my right; two bright stars just over the horizon were in front of me. I covered one eye, and tried to look where the telescope was pointing. The two bright stars were in the middle of my field of vision. I leaned back against the wall of his house and continued to stare, as he was staring. One of the stars seemed to be sparkling off and on; but the other had the dull, steady shine of a coin.

I knew I should turn home but I didn't want to. I edged away from his house and ran through his back yard to the thin trees behind. I heard a cry of some kind from the woods beyond, and couldn't tell if it was the sound of an animal, or maybe Jim cupping his hands around his mouth on the other side of the ravine. When I reached the back of Mrs. Richard's house, I veered off into the brush.

The branches of the trees were knitted together and blocked out the moonlight. I started walking half sideways so a twig wouldn't poke out my eye. Now and then I'd glimpse a star caught in the upper webbing of the trees.

When I cleared the woods, I heard a rushing sound. I could make out the slope going down into the ravine, and when I got to its edge, I found what was causing the sound. The warm weather must have melted off the last patches of snow, and rivulets everywhere were pouring down the slope. The creek at the bottom was usually a trickle, but all these little streams rushing into it had added together and made it into a torrent.

I descended carefully, facing the slope, using roots and small trees as handholds. But I slipped on a piece of slate and slid a ways on my hands and knees before I found my footing on a small embankment. I caught my breath and looked carefully around, until I sighted the crooked path down the rest of the ravine, and a jam of trees and rocks where I could cross.

I made it all right up the far side. I could feel the wet on my knees from the one misstep; if it wasn't for that, you couldn't tell I'd had any trouble.

When I got to the shack, I knew I was all right because I could hear them laughing and talking. I knocked on the flimsy door and waited. Suddenly there was silence inside. Then the door crashed open and there was a light in my face, and I heard Keith saying, "What the bloody hell?"

I held out my hands to block the light. I could just

see him reach for my arm and pull me inside and close the door behind me.

"What do you want?" he asked roughly. The flashlight beam was waving around the darkness, bringing odd bits of things into color: a red-and-white pack of cigarettes, a silver lantern, one of Jim's blue eyes.

"Take it easy," said Jim. He was holding a lighter to a candle, and Robby switched on the dull green light of a three-way lantern.

"What *are* you doing here?" asked Keith again.

"He's got a telescope," I said.

"What?" said Keith.

"Harold," I said.

"You'd expect a Martian to have a telescope," said Robby.

"Yeah, but it's strange," I said. I glanced at Jim. "He's looking at something."

"Uh-huh," said Keith. He was trying to smile, as he had the first time I'd been to the shack, but he wasn't pulling it off.

"I don't know what yet," I said.

"Okay," said Keith. "You go on ahead and find out." He stayed standing, while Jim sat down on the crate. "And then come back. Come back and tell us." Keith was nodding, and it reminded me of the way I'd seen him speak to teachers.

I stood there a moment longer—I could feel my shoulders sag. Then I started to turn around.

"Wait a minute," said Jim. "The kid's trying. Aren't you?" His face was partly lit by the flickering candlelight.

I nodded.

"Keith is just a little rude," said Jim, "because we were about to go on a mission."

"No mission," said Keith. To Jim he said, "Drop it."

Jim looked slowly over at Keith, and then back at me. "How'd you like to come along?"

"Dammit," said Robby.

Keith stood up and walked into the dark part of the shack. When he came back into the light, his face was set. "It's just not the right time. Thanks about the telescope. You're doing good."

"What do you think?" asked Jim.

I looked from Keith—whose eyes were averted—to Jim, and shrugged. "What the hell," I said.

"All right," said Jim, and he grinned at the other two.

Robby started for the door, walking past me. "You're all covered in mud," he snapped.

We took a shortcut I didn't know about, which seemed to be heading toward Wagoner Road. It was a grassy patch with two tire tracks, perhaps an old Jeep road. We were running slowly, and I made myself keep up, even after I got a pain in my side. When we came out on Wagoner, lights from a car were heading toward us, and we ran into a lawn far outside their beams.

Now we were walking quickly down Wagoner; I figured they didn't want to run, not so much because they were tired, but so as not to attract attention if someone happened to glance up from his newspaper. I wasn't sure where we were going until we came to the house that was being built. There were places for windows in the walls; much of the black tar paper had been covered over by wooden siding that reflected the dull yellow light of the moon.

"Here we are," said Keith under his breath. Then they ran toward the house and fanned out, like troops going into a village.

I waited outside for a moment. Then I heard a dull thudding sound and ran toward it, up the unfinished brick steps, and into the house.

I was in what was probably going to be the living room, but it was hard to tell. The only roof above me was the sky. I heard the thudding again, and edged through what was going to be a wall but was now just a fence of two-by-fours. I walked through another half-completed wall, and then through a doorway.

In the dimness I made out a figure beating a piece of lumber against something dark and almost invisible, leaving ragged white marks on it. I stepped closer: it was Keith, smashing into one of the black tar-papered walls with a two-by-four. He must have been ripping into it with a sharp edge of the wood, for bits of fuzzy material came out like the insides of an enormous stuffed animal. I watched for a moment—he didn't seem to notice I was there—and then I walked back the way I had come.

I turned into what was going to be a hall, and into another room that opened around me. Pretty soon a kid my age would be living here—the family would be sitting right where I was, with iced drinks and magazines, maybe with a model of a ship on a table.

I walked toward a giant shell—it became an overturned wheelbarrow—and then through another doorframe, into an area of the house where the wall frames hadn't yet been put up. Off to one side were three silver rods sticking up, and something like a snake that Robby was pulling on as if his life depended on it. He saw me and cried, "Give me a hand!" I ran up and grabbed on to it—it was a slippery black tube with folds throughout to make it flexible. We both yanked at it a couple of times, but it was slick and hard to hold on to, and must have gone deep into the ground.

"Damn," he called under his breath, and then stood up to see what else he could do.

Now Jim appeared. He seemed to be making a kind of tour of the doorframes of the house. But instead of walking through as one normally would, he'd stop halfway—between one room and another—and then kick at the frame until pieces of the light-colored wood splintered off like the spears of a firework. He did it to the room entrance where I'd been with Robby; now he was doing it to the large room I'd come from. I pictured the same people with their iced drinks, but now it was as if the house had been shelled, for the doors hung crookedly; even the model ship was listing.

I turned and maybe to get that picture out of my head I kicked at the nearest wall. But I misjudged the distance in the dark and my foot hit the wood halfway into my kick and almost knocked me over. I felt myself getting mad at the house, as if the wall had kicked me. I took a step back and booted the wall again and again. Jim slowly pivoted his head toward me, like we were undersea. I really hadn't done anything, except try to pull on that tube. There was a pile of stones at the end of the room. I picked one up and felt it cut into my hand. It was a brick and I heaved it at the wall. It made a thud that sounded far away and then bounced off, splitting in two.

A second later, there was a burst of light. I couldn't see Jim, but whatever it was, it had turned Robby and Keith to statues. Then they took off, and I leaned over and stared through a glassless window. A porch light and spotlight had come on in the old man's house next door.

I ran for the road at first, but realized I was alone, and that the three of them were running in the other direction, heading for the sparse woods behind the house. I heard the old man's front door opening as I tore between the two houses. I made it into the woods and followed after their shapes. We were running behind houses now, parallel to Wagoner; dogs were barking, and it seemed as if house lights were going on in a line behind us, like a lit fuse trailing in our path. I put on an extra burst of speed and narrowed some of the distance between them and me.

We came out at the end of my street, a row of quiet houses with lamps and televisions on inside. They were doubled over—breathing hard and laughing.

"Here he is," said Jim. "You looked like you were trying to kick through that wall."

My side was aching; I pulled for breath, as if I'd been in some strange world, where there was hardly any air.

"Some definite police action on that one," said Keith. He sounded excited.

"Oh, let's go back," said Jim. "I do so love the bloody red lights . . ." He paused and Keith stared at him; then they both laughed and Robby and I joined in.

"You know you can't tell anyone," Keith said suddenly to me.

"I know," I said. I had seen his father yell at him once in his driveway, when he missed a catch. I didn't want to think what kind of trouble Keith would be in with him for this.

"Not any of your little friends," said Robby.

"He knows," said Jim. "Did a good job."

"I thought we might pull out that pipe," I said to Robby.

"You were trying to pull out the septic pipe?" said Keith. "That's the pipe for the *toilet!* Gross, get away, get away." Keith and Jim were laughing again, and Robby was rubbing his hands on his jacket.

"Let's go," said Robby.

"Yeah, we'd best split up," said Keith.

They ran off then, like ghosts. I stared in the direction they'd gone. Then I started walking down my street.

There were no lights on at Harold's house, but the porch light was on at mine. It never usually was. I stood by our mailbox for a moment, running my hand through my hair to comb out the burrs and leaves, slapping my pants legs to get off the mud that had caked on.

The door opened almost immediately when I rang the doorbell. "We've been worried about you," said my mother's voice. Standing in the glare of the porch light, I couldn't see inside.

"It's okay," I said, and walked into the house. My

mother was right in front of me, and my father was standing over by the couch smoking a cigarette. For a moment, they both appeared to be strangers: a tall woman with wells of shadow under her eyes; a man with a point of flame in his mouth.

"I'm sorry, I should have told you," I said. "I . . . I was over there—at Harold's house. He has this telescope." I tried to smile. "We could see space."

EIGHT

Harold didn't ride the bus the following day—Tuesday. I wasn't even sure he was in school. He could have been sick. So I walked home alone in the afternoon, with Keith and Robby and Jim ahead of me this time, still pretending they didn't know me, even as we passed the house we'd raided. We never usually saw the workers, but they were there now, along with some guy in a suit with a clipboard. You couldn't see much of what had happened from the street, but they could. I slowed down; one guy was shaking his head as he stood inside a doorframe that Jim had shattered. I must have been looking too hard, because a dirt clod stung my arm. Up the road, Keith was facing me. I walked quickly past the house. I was sure none of the workmen had noticed me, but I suddenly felt that the boy I thought was going to live there would never move in now.

During my lunch hour on Wednesday I managed to get permission to go to the library. Miss Harris was the librarian. She was a gray-haired lady about whom there were a couple of rumors. One was that she had been engaged to an Englishman before the war; the other was that she used to pose nude for paintings. As I walked in, she was copying something from the back flaps of books onto little white cards.

"Excuse me," I said. "But I'm looking for a map."

"Atlases," she said.

"Of the sky," I said. "Of a particular part of the sky."

She thought for a moment and then nodded crisply.

"This way," she said, and led me to a rack of newspapers that had long wooden rods through them, so they could be read like magazines.

"One doesn't expect to find such useful things in the newspaper ordinarily," she said as she turned the large pages.

"Other than the comics," I said, and she smiled a little.

"Yes, here we are. 'The Sky Above Us.' "

We were in one of the sections of the newspaper I didn't usually open; in the upper right-hand corner of the page was a chart in the shape of a large circle, like a clock face, sprinkled with dots. Some of the dots were connected with lines as in a little kid's puzzle book. The words "North," "East," "South," and "West" were written around it.

"Quite a good one, actually," she said.

"I guess."

"You see, these are constellations." She was tracing the lines between the points which showed figures—a bull, a bear. "If one just looks at the sky, at first it's a confusing mass of stars. But if one studies it, certain patterns emerge: constellations."

"Which one is that?" I asked.

"Orion," she said, tracing her finger over the three stars to which I'd pointed that formed what seemed to be the belt of a man, from which his arm and sword and legs radiated. "Named for a hunter in Greek mythology," she went on. "Met a bad end, as I recall— stung by a scorpion, or some such. Now, all along here—this thin dotted line—is the Milky Way." She straightened up as if she had finished.

There was hardly anyone else in the library, just the rows of empty tables.

"I'm still not sure . . ." I started.

"How's that?"

"Well, let's say I was looking in a certain direction— say almost directly south." I knew that was the direction heading toward the dead end of our street—in the fall there were flocks of birds streaming over. It was in that direction Harold had been gazing.

"All right," she said.

"And let's say it was—oh, like 6:30, let's say. In the evening. Can you tell from that chart what I was looking at?"

She pursed her lips. Perhaps what I was asking was too much trouble: she'd had some sort of tough life, losing her boyfriend in the war, maybe getting caught with her clothes off.

"If you can't . . ." I began.

"Now, let's see." She squinted at the fine print under the circle. "It says that this chart shows the night sky at 8:00 p.m. That's not so far off. But if . . . Excuse me, please." I stood back, freeing the end of the newspaper, and she shifted the entire page. The circle turned like a dial. "There now. Perhaps we have it."

I tilted my head to be able to read it.

"No, no," she said. "Look straight on it. See—there's what you saw. There's your planet." She touched her finger to a large black spot.

I read the name to myself as if it were a password.

Again that afternoon Harold didn't ride the bus home. The Buick, which his father usually took to work, was in the driveway of his house as I walked past. Maybe Harold was getting a ride home, but I couldn't understand why. Anything unusual with his car now made me curious: I was starting to wonder if its comings and goings had anything to do with the reason he had locked himself inside it that day.

Before I even changed out of my school clothes, I sat in the chair next to our bookcase and pulled out the thin volume of the *World Book* encyclopedia that I needed. As I sat there with the book propped in my lap, turning through its pages, my mother breezed past with her sewing basket and said, "That's good, Donald." I nodded; I had been there the evening the salesman had visited our home and told my parents how the purchase of the set would help me get into college.

After my mother left, I paused for a moment, on a page that had a picture of a woman without arms. Actually, she was a statue; somewhere between the time she'd been sculpted and then found again and put in a French museum, she'd been shattered in that way.

I flipped past her, to the section of the planet named after her.

Venus.

The second planet in the solar system, between Mercury and Earth, 25.9 million miles away. I read about its atmosphere and surface temperature, about its orbit and the length of its year, and I tried to remember some of the ancient stories about it. I thought those in particular might be something he'd like.

Thursday I didn't see him during the school day. I was starting to worry that he was really sick or perhaps had transferred away again, following his father to another car dealership. I almost asked David or Rich if something had happened to him, but I didn't want them thinking I was trying to be his friend or anything. I had to remind myself that I usually didn't see him during the school day. He was probably there, somewhere, with his head buried in a book.

As I climbed into the bus to go home, I found him sitting in the little front seat next to the door. I broke into a smile. He didn't act like he noticed me, and I was glad of that—it meant he hadn't changed during his absence.

There was an empty seat two behind his, so I grabbed it, even though it was always more fun to sit farther back in the bus, where the kids jumped up and down on the seats when we hit a bump, or leaned way back when we got to a hill and Mrs. Shaw, our driver, had to downshift—as if we could really make it harder for the bus to climb. But that seemed like silly stuff to me today.

I alternated between watching scenery and the back of his head. He never glanced to one side or the other—not even when we passed the volunteer fire truck; not even when Mrs. Shaw cut a corner too sharp and the right rear of the bus dipped as the back wheel went off the pavement, and the little kids screamed.

At our stop, Harold was out of the bus even as Mrs. Shaw pulled back the crank with her gloved hand. I had to push past an older girl from some other street who was coming out of the seat across from mine.

"You little jerk," she said, but I didn't care.

I wanted to be right behind him when we left the bus, so I could easily catch him on the road.

I needn't have worried; he was standing just a couple of steps ahead, by the side of the street, holding his hand to his forehead. When I drew up to him, he started walking, but not as quickly today.

"Where have you been?" I asked.

He took a few steps more. "I've been bus sick," he said. He did look pale.

"I guess that's like being car sick," I said, and as soon as I said it, I wondered if that was the reason he was sitting in the car that day. Trying to cure himself of it.

"I don't get car sick," he said. "That's why my mother drives me home."

"I guess the bus is a lot bumpier," I admitted. Well, at least I knew why he hadn't been on the bus, why the Buick was there in the afternoons.

We walked without speaking for a ways, past the ranch houses, past the old man's house, the house that was once again being built. All the way up the road I could hear the workmen—who were now staying late—driving in nails, starting out slow and then hitting their hammers with more speed and force as they pounded them home. It made a hollow feeling in my stomach.

"So, is anything new?" I finally said as we turned onto our street.

There was the slightest shake of his head.

"Not with me, either," I said. "Just some book report I'm doing, on this book about the planet *Venus.*" I stretched my arms and looked over at him as we walked, but he didn't seem to register what I'd said.

"It's pretty interesting and stuff," I went on. "You know, how it's got this thick layer of clouds of carbon doxide."

"Dioxide," he said.

"Yes, *dioxide.*" I nodded to him, as if we were teammates. His eyes were fixed ahead, his arms were pumping. He had picked up his pace.

"And the surface temperature," I said. "That's really something. Even though it's called Earth's twin, it's not, not really. Only in size. But the surface temperature—wow—100 C."

"C?"

"You know, capital C. And there's this neat thing—even though it's usually 25 million nine hundred thousand miles away, when it's closest to the earth, during, um, during this thing, then it's only 22 million sixty thousand miles. Pretty soon, it'll happen again, this thing, and it'll be closest to the earth since 1823!" He kept looking ahead, and I was panting a little from talking while we walked so fast, and from making up the figures I couldn't quite remember.

"And the year," I went on. "I mean the orbit—well, of course that's how they figure the year—it's 225

Earth days. But its day—one rotation—is once every thirty days!" We took two steps, stride for stride. "But the really interesting stuff, the really really interesting stuff was how a long time ago people didn't know that Venus was both the morning star and the evening star. They thought it was two different heavenly bodies. They called the one at night Hesperus, and the one in the morning Lucifer—hey, like the Devil—when all the time it was the same planet, just the same planet with these two different sides . . ."

Suddenly we were almost at his mailbox, and I looked angrily at it, as if it were some visitor that had interrupted us, ruining my chances to get him to talk. "So," I said, "so what do you think?"

"Think?"

"About Venus!"

He shrugged.

"Listen," I said, "I don't understand you. You get bus sick—I bet that is the same as car sick." I paused. "*Is* that why you were sitting in the car that day?"

"When?" he asked. His mouth immediately went still as he said that one clipped word. He was eyeing me through his glasses.

"The day with my dog—is that why you were there, to . . . to get over it?"

He shook his head rapidly, back and forth.

"And why—" His face was turned in profile, his lips looked sewn shut. "Why'd you get so scared of Chief that day?"

He shook his head. "Maybe I wasn't scared."

"Well, you seemed like it," I said, "and you shouldn't have been. It was just a dog."

"The great dog," he murmured.

"Now, listen here," I said. "He was—he is a good dog." I remembered Robby slamming his hand into the wall of the shack; Harold's glasses would probably break just at the nosepiece.

"That's not what I meant," Harold said softly. There was red rising in his face, the first time I'd seen that. "It's just that I was thinking—about something— something else—and then all of a sudden he was there—he, he fit into my thoughts."

"He fit into your thoughts? What thoughts?"

He quickly shook his head, as if he were frightened, as if he'd gone too far. "I can't explain. Just forget it, just forget I said anything."

"Okay," I said. "Okay." I still felt like hitting him for what he had said.

He shook his head again. Then he strode up his drive-way. Halfway to his house, he turned around. In a quiet voice that I could hardly hear—there were birds chirping in the trees above us—he said, "C means Celsius. It's way too hot. Nothing could ever live on Venus." He turned again and continued up his drive-way, and I watched him until he reached his front door and disappeared in the dark of his house.

NINE

I told my mother I'd be needing to stay after school to do work in the library for a few days—for a report on entomology—and would have to take the activity bus home. Once again I had the mixed-up feeling of being closer to what I was after and at the same time hopelessly far away. Most nights I sat on my desk and observed his house. My perch was more comfortable: I hadn't bothered with my pennies in weeks, so I'd scraped them into a coffee can. I'd watch his light go off and on. Whenever it went off, I tried to find excuses to go outside, to leave my parents watching the blue glow of the television screen. I usually said I was going to check on Chief; I'd walk out back and then around front, down the black ribbon of our asphalt driveway, and gaze up at the sky.

If he was just interested in astronomy, just in any star or planet, he could take his telescope out in the middle of his yard and survey the heavens. When I turned with my back toward his house and looked in the direction I thought he was looking, I could see the two bright lights—and then so many others. If his telescope moved one inch, how many more stars would he have in focus? And how many could he see through the lens that I couldn't locate with my eyes? The answer was *there;* the answer was hidden among the millions of lights in the sky.

After school, in the quiet of the library, I checked the star chart in the *Cleveland Press,* and Miss Harris showed me where to find books that would give me more information about various stars and planets.

Because I'd struck out on Venus, and because there didn't seem to be any other planets in the immediate neighborhood, I decided to focus on stars.

The first night after school I started with Betelgeuse, perhaps because it sounded like it had a connection with insects. I was wrong again here, too; the "beetle" in its name had nothing to do with entomology, but was actually from some Arabic words, *Ibt at Jauzah,* which meant "the giant's shoulder." The giant was Orion, the hunter in the constellation, who had met a bad end. I read about Betelgeuse anyway, and learned some about stars in general. The relative brightness of stars as seen from Earth was measured by something called "apparent magnitude." The lower the number, the brighter the appearance of the star. Betelgeuse had an apparent magnitude of about .5, which meant it was one of the brightest stars in the night sky.

Over the next several nights I read interesting stuff about other stars and constellations. One late afternoon seemed to drift into the next. The library was usually pretty empty at this hour; sometimes there would be small groups of kids sitting at various tables, surrounded by opened books, working on reports for one class or another. I read about Rigel—also in the constellation of Orion—a blue-white supergiant. I shifted to another nearby constellation, Gemini, and read about its twin stars, Castor and Pollux. They were named after twin brothers in Greek mythology, one of whom was mortal, one divine. When Castor, the mortal one, was stabbed to his heart, his brother, Pollux, would not leave him behind.

I read general information on the stars, too: about absolute magnitude, about different categorizations by size and color, about the Arabian and Greek astronomers who gave many of them their names.

But I still wasn't getting it. There was a group of fourth-grade girls at the two back desks of the library as I made my way to my usual place. I could hear them laughing and trying to make themselves quiet, and then breaking out in louder laughter. I opened the newspaper and stared at the day's atlas of the planets and stars. The laughter and whispered talking of the girls sounded a long way off as it rose and fell. For a moment I felt I was in one of those big observatories, with stone walls and tiled floors where footsteps echoed, and that the newsprint chart before me was the vault of heaven.

"Mr. Halley?"

I looked up suddenly and saw metal-colored hair, two eyes floating behind wavy glass.

"Are you all right?"

"Yes, I'm sorry," I said. "I guess I was lost in my thoughts . . ."

"My bad joke," said Miss Harris. "Edmund Halley, the famous astronomer."

"Right," I said, and only had to think a moment. "Halley's Comet."

She smiled. "The very one. And have you found what you wanted? You've been quite at it."

"Well, almost," I said, and then felt the tiredness in my shoulders, from hunching over these books, and from something else as well. This wasn't working. I could read up on every star in the heavens and I wouldn't know which one he was looking at, or even if he was looking for one. Maybe he observed a different star every night, and so what? So what? I could imagine Keith saying, and Robby saying, Why don't you just break his telescope? It all seemed stupid, and I started to close the book in front of me. Keith had been right all along; the only way to find out about him was for him to tell me, for me to be his friend, and even though I'd tried, and come as close as I ever could have wanted, he was just too hard to figure. Their strange idea, their illegal psychology experiment, just wouldn't work with everybody. I would have to tell them that. I'd have to hear them say, Well, nice try, kid, and see Robby smirk, and from then on, even if I wanted to, the closest I would ever get would be maybe to walk past their shack one day and see the flimsy wooden door shut on its hinges.

Miss Harris was talking to me, but I had only been hearing the murmur of her voice, the sound of the creek you crossed at the bottom of the ravine. ". . . Such interesting names," she was saying, "Procyon, Betelgeuse, Arcturus . . . and those are just the stars. The constellations, too." My eyelids began to feel heavy.

"Orion, the hunter, of course; and Gemini, the twins; and Taurus, the bull." She was running her finger over the star chart, like a small craft moving through the blackness of space. "Ursa Major, Boötes, Leo . . . And Canis Minor, and Canis Major, the Great Dog . . ."

"What did you say?" I asked too loudly. The girls at the end tables were looking over.

"Ursa Major," she said, in an even softer voice, reminding me to speak quietly. "You know they also call it the Big Bear."

"No. That's very interesting, but no. The 'Can—' one."

"Canis Minor. The Lesser Dog, I believe. And Canis Major."

"And Canis Major is . . ."

"The Great Dog."

I pictured Harold before me, his lips moving, the red rising on his face. "That's it," I said.

"Supposed to be one of Orion's hunting dogs. Canis Minor is the other."

"His hunting dogs," I said. "And the stars?" I was having trouble keeping my voice low. "The stars in those constellations?"

"Procyon," she said. "It means, let's see, 'Before the Dog.' And Sirius," she added, the same time I located it in the star chart. It could have been one of the two I'd seen that first night.

"Sirius," she said again, and I felt my heart surge. "I believe it's known as the Dog Star."

At home that night, I was restless. My father said during dinner that my feet couldn't stop moving, and during a TV show I usually liked I left twice to get a glass of water in the kitchen and stare into the darkness of our back yard.

Sirius.

I knew I would try it a different way this time, and if I was right, it might work. And then maybe I would find out something else about him—maybe he was afraid of it—and maybe then we would have our snake. It could be just another dead end . . . but this time I would let him tell me.

Before it was time for me to go to bed, I went to say good night to Chief.

Even though it was cool out, I didn't put on my jacket. I walked through the trees in our back yard, stepping around their shapes as they loomed before me in the darkness, each one a mute, separate world.

Chief rattled his chain and barked as I approached. I patted his head and chest, and then I unhooked him with my left hand. With my right, I grabbed his collar. And then for a moment I stood there with him—he was panting, like he wanted to run, as he used to. I thought about Orion and his dog, who were hunters together. I walked around him, until I got just the right angle, until I could see the neighbor's back-porch light shining red and yellow from his eye like a star.

TEN

An exploding star is a nova, which is Latin for "new." It's called that because when a faint sun has expanded and brightened in this way, it may seem to us on Earth as if a star has appeared out of nowhere.

After the nova in the library with Miss Harris, I spent nearly two weeks trying to maneuver Harold into talking. Two weeks of looking through star books so I knew which innocent things to say; two weeks of watching the lights go out and then quickly on in his bedroom; of not wanting to run into Jim or Keith or even Robby until I had more from Harold about his closely guarded subject; of being jumpy during dinner and my father noticing how my feet could never stop moving, even as I ate my Swiss steak or meat loaf. And two weeks of walking home from school with him, convincing him it wasn't math, it wasn't bugs, it wasn't coins, it wasn't even Venus—it was the *stars*, the stars I was interested in.

I told him how incredible it was that long ago people hadn't known much about the heavens, how they'd thought that planets and stars were the same thing. I had to pause then and stop myself from smiling, because that was the mistake I'd almost made with Harold.

They'd finally observed that the stars didn't move among themselves, but the planets did, I said. "In fact, 'planet' comes from a Greek word that means 'wanderer.' " I was sure he knew most of this, but I felt I had to let him know I was a good student, a good apprentice, someone worthy.

One afternoon I caught him after we'd gotten off the bus, and breathlessly told him that the sun, which was classified as a Yellow Dwarf, would someday expand and cool to become a Red Giant. "And the really interesting thing," I said, "the really really interesting thing is how it seems so bright to us but it's really a little speck in the middle of the vast darkness of the universe"—a phrase I'd memorized from a book—"and that other far-off stars are really much brighter."

He favored me with a look. "Of course, that's the difference between apparent and absolute magnitude," he said.

"Of course. And all these other stars are so much brighter," I said again. We were halfway down our street—smoke was curling from the chimneys of the houses around us, Mrs. Miller in her bathrobe was putting up the little flag on her mailbox—and my mouth went suddenly dry. "But what is the brightest star, then?" I asked. "As it appears to us. I mean, besides the sun."

He stared ahead again and I thought I'd lost him.

"Sirius," he said softly.

"Really?" I said. "Too bad we can't see it from up here, up in this part of the world."

"Of course we can see it," he said, and he seemed almost angry.

"Then what I wouldn't give," I said, "to be able to look through a telescope at that particular star."

I was quiet the rest of the way home. Waiting, like a boy lying in the grass with a string tied to a belt, and if you only tugged it just the right amount . . . But he didn't say another thing.

The next afternoon I was off again. The only way I knew to go forward was to wear him down.

"The reds are really the coolest temperature," I said. "Of course, they're really really hot, but compared to the others . . ." He was squinting ahead. "Then, of course, there are the yellow stars, which are somewhat warmer. Like the sun. Blue stars are the hottest, and below them are the white stars." I knew that Sirius was a white star. "White stars are as hot as 35,000 degrees Fahrenheit." This number was twice as large as it should have been. He blinked once, but he didn't correct me. "It's because there are these different wavelengths of light," I continued. "Like if you see a piece of metal heated, it will turn red, then white . . ." and on and on and on . . .

That night I was lying on the floor of the living room, reading the comics, when Chief started barking. My mother kept reading her book, but my father quickly lowered his newspaper. He kept it lowered while Chief barked several more times, probably at a squirrel; when he stopped barking, my father lifted the paper slowly back up. He had been looking at the supermarket ads—I caught a glimpse of them upside down—probably comparing the prices of the competition to those charged at his store.

Suddenly I heard the rebel yell from our back yard. It seemed pretty close to our house, and it set Chief to barking again.

"I'll find out what's up with Chief," I said, and went to the door.

It was another chilly night. A few stars shone through the upper leaves of our trees, but I couldn't see them well enough to tell which ones they were. Halfway back to Chief's little house, I felt somebody grab me from behind and pin both my arms.

"Hey!" I said.

Jim came out from behind our big forked tree and gave me a light tap on the stomach. It must have been in exactly the right place, because it knocked the wind out of me; then I felt a burning sensation in my belly. I coughed a little, but tried not to show anything on my face.

Keith let me go and came around in front of me.

"So, what's new?" he asked.

"Really good stuff," I said. I could still feel a finger of pain reaching across my gut.

"Like?"

I glanced at Jim. He was wearing one of the junior letterman's jackets they gave the eighth-graders; sewn to an L were insignias of a bat and ball, and a football.

Jim nodded toward the back of our lot, and Keith and I started back there with him.

"So this is the dog," said Jim.

Chief was standing on his three good legs, with his back paw slightly off the ground. His tail was twitching a little, and his eyes were on me.

"It's okay, boy," I said.

"Just call him tripod," said Keith.

"Oh, shut up," said Jim.

I put my hand out to Chief. "It's okay," I said again.

"So?" Keith shrugged. I couldn't tell if he was interested or bored.

"Where's Robby?" I asked.

"Homework," said Keith. "Two of his brothers flunked math, and his old lady's making him stay in so he doesn't."

I grinned. Robby had three brothers close to him in age; kids always joked that his parents got them mixed up.

"We just need to know if anything's going on. This is dragging. Other things are coming up."

"A lot's going on," I said. "I had to go to the library to double-check some of it."

"You're kidding," said Keith, and laughed. "And what about old Miss Harris? Did she have her clothes on?"

"She did." Jim was smiling. "But you know, I almost asked her which was better, a telescope or the naked eye."

"That's rich," said Keith. "You know Harrelson got caught trying to draw her that way."

"Really," I said. "What I wouldn't give to see that."

All three of us were laughing now. Then they grew quiet, and I did, too.

"So?" said Keith.

"Wait till you hear," I said. "At first, I thought it would be bugs—he had this kind of thing with insects."

"That would be good," said Keith.

"But it's better than that," I said. I looked from one to the other. "It seems he has this, this kind of weird interest in a star."

"On which show?"

"Not that kind," I said. "Not from Hollywood. A star—up in the sky. Sirius. I think he's got his telescope trained on it. I think he knows all about it—how it's the brightest star, and how it's white-hot, and what its temperature is, and . . . and everything." I tried to think what else I had, but I could only come up with the facts on the stars that I had told to him. Chief was looking at me, his right eye shining red. "There is something about it," I said. "He does have some strange thing about it . . ." I trailed off. I suddenly felt it was just scraps of ideas and weird feelings that I had built into something—it was like a vivid dream that loses its color by the time you get to the kitchen for breakfast, and later in the day you can't even remember it.

They didn't say anything.

Keith shook his head. "Just keep it up. And be sure and tell us everything you find out about . . . Sirius. Seriously." He snorted. Then he looked at Jim. "Let's bloody go."

"There is something," I said.

"Yeah," said Keith. "He's made you as lame as he is. Sorry, pup," he said to Chief, once again with his all-American smile.

I turned to Jim, but he was looking away, into the darkness of the other yards.

I couldn't believe it was over, just like that.

When I came back inside, my mother had left the room, and my father was sitting there alone, with the newspaper folded on his lap. There was a shot glass half-filled with whiskey next to the beer can on the table. He looked small, suddenly, with the couch stretching on both sides of him.

"It's okay," I said. "There never was anything out there." Then I had to quickly walk from the room.

ELEVEN

After the bus stopped, I waited around in the back until nearly everyone was off. The girl I'd cut in front of that one day wrinkled her nose at me as I stood and waited just behind her seat. Keith, Jim, and Robby hadn't ridden home today, but I knew it wasn't because they were trying not to see me or anything: it was because baseball practice was starting and they were all trying out for the eighth-grade team. Keith went out for pitcher, and I figured he'd make it, because his father spent so much time correcting the way he threw the ball and held the bat. Robby usually made the team, even if it was only second-string outfield. Jim was the third baseman, and there was no question there—he was quick at fielding, and although he wasn't a power hitter, he could be counted on to drive in a run when it mattered.

Kids were walking ahead of me in groups, some of them with their jackets half down their arms in the sun. Harold had looked quickly around the bus when it had stopped, and noticed that I was hanging around in the back. Then he had rushed off until he was way out in front, and I could walk my normal pace without catching up to him. I didn't want to take all afternoon to get home, because there was something I had to do.

There was that whole coffee can full of pennies that I had to go through.

That house was pretty near to being finished. The windows were in, the doors hung straight, I was sure the toilet flushed. You couldn't tell that we had done anything. They had even cleaned up the junk from the yard and raked it smooth.

When I turned down my street, I thought how the plan we had started had all burned down—it was cooling, from white, to yellow, to red—and whatever I had thought about Harold and my dog and that strange star would flicker down into gray, a cinder that Keith would kick out of his way.

Then I saw Harold standing on the street, just a little ahead of his mailbox. He seemed to be studying his house, its green siding, its scraggly lawn and closed garage door. The house looked as it usually did, but he was scrutinizing it as if he had never seen it before. Or seen it too many times.

When I reached him, he fell into step beside me. We were only a couple of paces from his drive—but in those few steps everything began to heat up again, red to yellow, and higher, because he gave me a quick glance out of the corner of his eye and said, "If you're really interested, I could sometime let you take a look at that star."

Three nights later, when I walked toward his house as he had said—on the next clear night—I thought I shouldn't be so surprised he had finally invited me in. Not just because of all the work I'd put in, but for another reason, too. If someone spends a lot of time looking at something in his room . . . and somebody, maybe anybody, else seems interested . . .

"You can put your eye up to it if you want," Harold said. "It's a small refractor, but you can see it."

I placed my eye to the telescope pointing from his opened screen, and the dim stars sprinkled before me suddenly sharpened and grew brighter.

"Don't jiggle it," he said. "Do you see that one, that's mainly white, but with different colors?"

"Yes." I was seeing a bright white star, with sudden red and yellow tints passing over it.

"That's it, and you were wrong. It's 17,500 degrees Fahrenheit." He paused. "I don't know why you're smiling. You can't miss it, the way I've got the lens pointed right at it."

He had no idea why I was smiling. The star before me was white now, and twinkling.

"Why does it turn different colors?"

"They say it's because of the earth's atmosphere. Because Sirius is such a southerly star, and so from up here, in the Northern Hemisphere, you see it through all the earth's air, which distorts the light." He was quiet for a moment. "Of course, there is scientific validity for that view. But there is this odd thing. This ancient Greek astronomer, Ptolemy, said it was a red star. So did the Egyptian astronomers. But then, in the tenth century, all the reports stated that it was a white star, and it's classified that way now."

My right eye was watering from staring, and my left

eye, which was shut, was starting to ache. Still, I watched Sirius, a shifting dog's eye.

"So how do they explain it?" I asked carefully, so as not to move the telescope. "Did it turn from red to white?"

"A star can't do that so quickly."

"So?" I asked again. I was holding my left eye shut with my hand, but my right eye was still watering. Sirius was dancing all over the sky.

"*They* don't," said Harold.

I moved away from the lens, and rubbed my eyes with my hands, making little sunbursts in the darkness of his room.

"It's really neat," I said.

He stared at me, without expression. There was a star map on the wall behind him, and his bald-looking head in front of it was floating in the midst of galaxies.

"It's not *neat*," he said, and clicked on a light. Now the stars behind him turned into dull points of white on a crinkled map thumbtacked to the wall. One leg of the telescope had a math book underneath it, to even it up.

Harold fell into an overstuffed chair he had against the wall next to his bed. He appeared small, sunken in the large cushions, and strange.

A moth had come in through the open screen, and was flying around the ceiling light.

His house had seemed pretty ordinary when he led me through it; the furniture that didn't match and the thin carpeting reminded me of a motel, but there was nothing really odd about it. His room was another story, and I was hopeful it would provide the kind of information I needed. It was a mess: there were open books strewn everywhere, and others unevenly stacked up. Many were about science and astronomy, and ranged from *Boys' Book of the Stars,* an oversized volume with lots of pictures in it, to a thick, cloth-covered book, *The Mathematics of Astronomy.* I suddenly wondered if he had read them all, and how dumb had I sounded when I spouted off what little I knew. Even so, it had gotten me here.

Socks and underwear were tumbling out of a drawer in a chest. There was a clown face on the light switch on the wall, which didn't seem to fit in at all, and high on one shelf was the lunch box with rockets and galaxies I'd heard about.

In addition to the star map, there was a chart of stars listed by absolute and apparent magnitude. There was also a map of the world, and some kind of poster I'd never seen before, which showed a person's hands in various positions. I walked over to it and silently read the caption: "International Language of the Deaf."

"Hey!" I said.

He looked quickly over at me.

I pointed to the chart. "So—what's this for?"

He stared at me a moment longer, and then, as if he was bored, he took a cookie from a paper bag in his pocket and started to eat it.

Over on his desk was a small wooden box with a glass top, and inside there were about twenty insects of different kinds—beetles, wasps, dragonflies, ants—pinned with little tags underneath them, and names written in Latin. It was entomology, and I felt a rush of pride.

I read a label underneath a grasshopper. *"Orthoptera Acridodae."*

"Acrid-di-*dae,"* he said. He still seemed bored.

I wandered over to the star map. The constellations were marked in faint lines. I saw Cassiopeia and Orion. Then I found the one I was looking for.

"Canis Major," I said.

He glanced at me.

"And there's Sirius," I said. "But what's this little dot next to it?"

He scooted to his bed and sat so his legs were hanging over the side of it. There *was* something in the way he was looking at me.

"That little dot next to it," I said again.

"That's Sirius B," he said after a moment. "Sirius is a binary star—that means it's got a companion. They discovered it because someone mapped Sirius's course and found it wobbled all over the place. As if it was wandering but it wasn't a planet . . ."

He was gazing off, at the empty wall in his room, not even at the maps, but it seemed at some chart behind his eyes. "The thing is," he said, "they didn't discover this companion star until 1844. If there was something smaller, they still wouldn't have seen it." He nodded slightly—as if to himself—and sat with his back against the headboard of his bed.

"What are you saying?"

He sat there silently, as if unwilling to go on. "See, if you were on Sirius," he said at last, softly, "and you had a huge telescope—say as big as the Palomar 200-inch reflector—and you looked through it at the sun, you wouldn't be able to see anything but the sun."

Although his voice was still soft, it was now higher—
he seemed both excited and trying not to be. "You
wouldn't be able to see Venus. Or Mars. Or even
Earth." He peered at the map of the world, but I felt he
meant everything around us, too: this room, the street,
his house and my house and the voices from the living
room. "Just the speck of light that would be the sun."
He started making a clicking sound with his tongue
against his teeth. Then he said, "So, if we were looking
at Sirius . . ."

"What?" I said.

He was staring again at the blank wall in front of
him, and then his gaze shifted to the telescope. I
watched him for a moment. Then, as if it was what he
wanted me to do, I walked over and put my eye to the
lens.

Sirius was there, blinking white, yellow, red. It
seemed to be flashing out a message I couldn't yet
read.

TWELVE

As I sat at my desk and put the pennies from the coffee can into rolls—hardly looking at them—I kept turning his comments over and over in my mind. If you were looking at Sirius and couldn't see something smaller than its companion star, and if someone from Sirius was looking at us and they couldn't make out Earth or the other planets, then . . . It didn't make any sense; it was like a math problem that had no solution. It was like the chart of the hands on his wall. Yet I found myself thinking about it, almost putting my finger on it, only to have it slip away. I made myself recall other facts I had read: that it was an important star to the ancient Egyptians, who figured their new year by its rising. That they called it Sothis. And how it seemed to herald to them a time when the floodwaters would come and save them, save their crops from scorching and dying . . .

Maybe Keith was right about me; maybe I was getting as strange as Harold. But I felt I'd been on to something all along, that there was something there, and I was close now. Not light-years—not even miles. But feet. Inches.

I didn't see Harold for two days, but I kept up the surveillance through my window. When I should have been doing my homework, I watched the Buick come and go; his mother walking in with her arms full of groceries and Harold carrying nothing; his father being dropped off in the evening by someone who drove an Oldsmobile, and before he strode up the driveway, past the scraggly grass, he would also stare up at the wide expanse of sky.

On the third day—it was a Thursday—Harold again didn't ride the bus. I figured he'd been bus sick all week, and might be tomorrow as well, which meant I might not be able to run into him again until Monday. Would he still feel like talking to me then?

But as I walked down my street—turning the words "Sirius," "Sothis" over and over in my mind—I saw him stepping down the drive from his house; it seemed as if he'd timed it to meet me, that he must have caught a glimpse of me from one of the windows on the other side of his house after he'd ridden home from school in their car.

He didn't pretend his being there was a coincidence. Beneath his small glasses, his eyes stayed fixed on me.

He said as I drew even with him: "My mom wants to know if you want to come in for some cookies."

I paused for a moment, and then nodded. I didn't want to appear—perhaps I didn't want to feel—too eager to get the rest of the story. But Jim, Keith, and

Robby were probably at that very moment scooping up grounders and wandering around beneath pop flies: they'd never have to know.

We walked up his front steps, and then he opened the screen door and the inside door. He looked down at a length of carpet that must have been put there to rub your shoes on, and he stepped over it. I followed him through the living room that I had seen before.

"Is that you?" Harold's mother called from the kitchen around the corner.

There was a yellow Formica table, and a row of pans and another row of potholders on hooks on the wall. There was a Betty Crocker cookbook open, and on a small shelf a *Good Housekeeping* cookbook and what looked like a textbook from some home-ec class, called *Serving Your Family Nutritious Meals*. Harold's mother was bringing out a tray of cookies from the oven. Her hair was teased up, she was wearing a sweater tucked into a skirt, and she had makeup on. She looked like a high-school girl you might hear a rumor about, disguised as a mom.

"And you brought Donald," she said, and smiled, and I saw again the fine lines around her mouth and eyes. Harold hadn't responded to either of the things she'd said, but she went on. "I've just finished this batch," she said. She put them on a rack on the table, and then took off the thick yellow oven mitten she was wearing that had the face of a dog stitched on it. She put it by Harold's face and said in a kind of babyish voice, "Does him want a cookie?"

Harold glowered at her, and her face went still and she put the mitten on a shelf.

"They sure look good," I said.

She lifted off cookies with a spatula and put two on each of our saucers. Then she sat down.

"You must have seen Harold's telescope," she said. "You know he begged and begged for so long for it that his grandparents just broke down and got it for him. His father says"—she smiled suddenly and looked young again—"that he wants to peek at the girls up and down the street." Her eyes looked stricken and she put her hand in front of her mouth—as she had that day I'd seen her cry through the window. I couldn't understand why this would make her cry. Then she brought her hand away and I saw she was trying not to laugh . . .

Harold narrowed his eyes and picked up a cookie from his saucer and studied it.

"I saw it," I said to his mother. "That and his signs for the deaf." I had the sudden thought that *she* was deaf and that that explained the strange tension I was feeling, maybe explained why she had laughed that day as well. It *would* be funny to see things and not really know what was going on. I looked at her, and then as I pointed down to my saucer I said in a way that made my lips clearly move, "These are good cookies."

"Well, you haven't tried one yet," she said. I broke off a piece of one and ate it. The dough wasn't quite cooked enough, but it was overloaded with nuts and chocolate chips. It was as if she was trying hard but hadn't quite got the hang of it.

I nodded encouragingly at her, which I figured covered me in both languages.

No one said anything for a while. She was now looking at Harold, who put the cookie back on his saucer.

93

"You have a really nice house," I said to his mother, and she acted as if she couldn't hear me.

"Aren't you gonna eat it?" she asked Harold.

Harold sat there a moment longer without responding. Then he took a brown paper bag out of his pocket and started putting one of his cookies inside.

"You know there's always plenty more," she said. But he ignored her. He was folding the bag over and over so the cookie was sealed within.

"I'll have another one," I said. She gave me the slightest smile—more a twitch, really—then stood up.

"I don't know why you have to ruin everything," she said to Harold. Her voice was uneven—as if there was a skip in a record—and she quickly turned and walked from the room.

He blinked once—but it was more like his whole face blinked, the bottom half of it crinkling up to meet his eyes.

He put the one cookie that remained on his saucer back on the rack.

He was gazing out, and I suddenly felt my anger for him. It was true what she said, that he ruined things: that afternoon with his father, this time with his mother. And that day in the car.

"She seems really nice."

He stared at me, through his little glasses. Then he sighed. "Come on," he said, and he stood up, and after a moment I followed him to his room.

His telescope was still by the window. In the light I could make out its three-legged base—a tripod—and my face felt hot for a moment. Little else in the room seemed changed, but the scope itself was in a different position. It was definitely pointed lower.

Harold flopped down on his bed and sat against the headboard with his arms folded.

I pointed to the telescope. "Peeking at the neighbors?"

"It's closer to the horizon," he said in a flat voice. "Its declination is -16.4 degrees—16.4 degrees south— so it never gets that high up here anyway. They're already getting good views of it on the other side of the world."

"Sirius?"

He nodded.

"Remember what you said, about not seeing it from up here, in the north?"

I nodded.

"It is true for part of the year," he said. He kept staring at me. "It's going away—I mean, it stops being visible now." Then, in a softer voice: "Maybe that's why I wanted you to see it."

"But it comes back," I said. "It's a star. It revolves or something."

"It's because of the earth's position compared to the sun," he said.

"That's what I mean."

He shook his head. "It's supposed to happen right around now," he said. "Or maybe just after it disappears—I think it differently different times."

"You mean there's a chance to get a really good look at it or something?" I was thinking of what he had said about the companion star, how hard it was to see . . .

"And then it will be . . . at least another year," he went on. "If not this year."

"What will be?"

He shook his head.

"What's supposed to happen?" I asked.

He bit his knuckle. "It's a dream," he said.

"Yes?"

"It was a funny time. I was little and there were all these things happening to me. I was looking at things, and numbers, and understanding them, and asking all kinds of questions, and no one knew what to think of me, and that I could do that. And then I started having this dream, I don't know why. How they came to visit me. When I wake up, I know it isn't real. But I . . . I think about it during the day sometimes."

The light glinted off one of his lenses.

"Who comes to visit?" I asked. "In the dream."

"I shouldn't think about this."

"Who?"

"From Sirius," he said. "From a planet system off Sirius."

"Come on," I said, before I could stop myself.

He was staring straight ahead again, not at me. Outside, the late-afternoon sun was streaming down; in a neighboring drive some girls were skipping rope. But here there was a map of the galaxies and a telescope, tracking a star.

I heard a knock at the door, and my heart began hammering in my chest.

"Harold," said his mother through the door, "your father's home." Her voice sounded even again.

He looked at me then, and I checked for a smile or a sudden laugh, or even a sign that his mother's voice had registered—but I knew I wouldn't see them.

"He'll be right there," I called to his mother, as I watched him. And all the while, until I reached over and opened the door, he did look like he belonged to another world.

THIRTEEN

The end of that week, on Saturday, the garage door stayed closed, the front curtains were shut, the Buick was nowhere in sight. All that day I could see no sign of life—they had gone off on one of their trips again. At dusk, from my window, I saw an older kid riding his bike fast up the street and staring over at Harold's house. I couldn't see where he had come from. He had brown hair slicked in the back like Jim's, but I had never seen Jim ride down our street. I couldn't get a good enough look to tell for sure who it was.

By Sunday, the Buick had returned. There was some fog in the early morning, but it was mostly gone by the time I noticed the blue car parked on the apron of their driveway.

After breakfast, I walked between the houses across from me, and then along the thin woods behind them till I was parallel with his house. I didn't see anything there, but I sat in the bushes and low trees and waited. It was not like I had much else to do.

After about a half hour in which I almost fell asleep sitting against a sweet-smelling tree, I heard a door bang. Harold came out and stood on the back steps. At first I thought it was a dream I was having myself. As I came fully awake I watched him walk down to the rear sidewalk with a bat and whiffle ball he was carrying.

He stood there a moment, glancing around. Then he tossed up the ball and swung at it. He missed again and again, but he picked it up each time and tossed it. He must have got about ten strikes before he took a nick out of the ball, and then it went spiraling behind him and almost hit his house. He picked it up and started trying again. He had the timing all wrong, and the bat looked as if it was too heavy for him: he sat it on his shoulders, and by the time he brought it up and swung it, the ball had already gone most of the way to the ground. The weight of the bat twisted his body almost in a circle.

It was funny to see—I knew he must be getting tired and frustrated—and I knew, too, if he hadn't given his father such a hard time with the golf he'd be out there now showing him how to do it. But after a while I didn't like watching it anymore, and I turned and walked quietly back through the woods toward my house.

On Monday, my father took the afternoon off from work, to wait for some men to come and work on our lawn. When I got home from school, there was a big tank truck in our driveway, and my father was talking to two fellows wearing gray overalls. I stood there awhile, but they were deeply involved in their conversation about aphids and dandelions. I went inside and sat on the couch by the picture window, and watched them. They were walking up and down the lawn, spraying fertilizer and bug killer from hoses that snaked from the truck, wearing masks that made them look like they weren't human.

That night I knocked on Harold's front door, and he let me in without saying a word. I felt he'd been expecting me.

He sat down on his bed, and I went to his window and pushed the curtain aside. I could see Orion. I could pick out Betelgeuse and Rigel.

"It's interesting about Sirius B," he said.

"Oh?"

"The companion star to Sirius. You remember. You know they call it the Pup?"

"Neat," I was starting to say, but he went on.

"It's a white dwarf. That means it's super dense. It's collapsed onto itself. Its matter has seventy thousand times the density of water, which means if you took a matchbox of it and brought it down to Earth, that small amount would weigh more than a ton."

He said nothing for a moment. Then: "It's nine light-years away."

"Sirius B?"

"Sirius. That means when we see it now we're seeing it the way it was nine years ago, because it's taken the light nine years to get here. Now if a light-year is six million million miles, and you multiply that by nine . . ."

"Nine years ago," I said. I looked out the window, but Sirius was out of sight. "That would be what it looked like when we were two years old."

99

He stared at me, his face not registering.

"You know, nine years ago," I said. "If we're eleven now. You're the math whiz."

After a moment he said, "No one's sure, but they don't think anything can travel faster than that." He half closed his eyes. "It would have to be a circular craft."

I glanced over at his desk. Maybe I would see science-fiction magazines strewn about. There weren't any.

"Circular?"

"As you approach the speed of light, your mass increases, and your time slows down. Basic Einsteinian theory. If the craft was circular, or based on spherical shapes, it would withstand the outward pressure. It would be like a ripple on a pond," he said. "Growing, without breaking, and then of course it could tighten again . . ."

I was standing by the telescope, and I put my hand out to touch it, perhaps to get a sense of steadiness.

"Try not to move that," he said.

I nodded.

"Now, you say nine years," he said. "If they left eight years ago, it would be next year . . ." He seemed to think of something, and went on. "But if you're on the craft, it wouldn't be like that. If you're on the craft, time slows down. Say you leave on a space journey yourself, at the speed of light. When you return, you think you've only been gone a couple of years. You're only a couple of years older."

"Thirteen," I said.

"But your parents," he said.

"What about them?"

"Well, when you return—they've gotten terribly old. Even if you're still a kid, it wouldn't be the same. Maybe they've gone deaf, and, and they can hardly see you." He paused.

"Why?" I asked.

"You see, sixty years of regular time have gone by." His voice was steady again. "But when you're near the speed of light, it's only a couple of years . . . But they might adjust for that," he said. "Of course they would. They wouldn't let themselves be surprised by things like that."

He scrambled off the bed.

"In my dream, they would know about the Earth. How it could support life. But they would wonder if anyone was here, what we were like. And they would want to stop at other planets on the way. On Uranus. On Saturn. On Mars. When I was littler we were on this vacation by Lake Erie and my parents . . ." He blinked his face again. "We were in this cottage and you could hear everything. And there was this fly in the room, and you could hear him. My parents had put me on this cot to take a nap, and maybe they thought I could sleep, but I couldn't. So I listened to him in the afternoon: he'd buzz to the cookie jar, and then to the apples sitting out, and then to the refrigerator door . . . I kept thinking how they'd be able to land on different worlds like that if they wanted to."

He glanced quickly over at the map.

"And they come . . . here?" I said. "I mean, in your dream."

"Yes," he said, and then went back and sat on his bed, with his feet dangling over the side.

"It would be all worked out," he said. "Their map wouldn't be anything like this, of course. It might just be numbers, but they could read it like a map. They would see the town and the school, the streets and where the bus lets us off, and the houses." He looked at me. "Your house. And the field behind, and the woods behind mine.

"And they'd be looking for an intelligent being," he said. "It might be hard to tell at first. They might have an idea what to expect, if they had studied us through their telescopes. But there would be other ways. They could look to see if the being they approached was wearing something manufactured. Not just fabric— that could be grown. But if the Earth person had some kind of metal or glass on them, then they would know to try and communicate. Like a belt buckle. Like a watch. Maybe they'd walk up to a dog on a leash, but they'd figure it out quickly enough . . ."

He flicked his eyes at me and away. There was a little spot of red on each cheek.

"So, if they approached you, you'd have to show you were in fact intelligent. Maybe by drawing lines in the dirt. Addition: first one mark. Then two. Then three. Multiplication: one mark. Then two. Then four, then eight. Cubes: two marks. Then eight. Or maybe other ways."

"What if they aren't friendly?" I asked suddenly.

He knotted his forehead, as if the thought had never crossed his mind. "You'd have to show them *you* were," he said. He shook his head. "They won't mean any harm. They'll just be curious."

"What will they look like?" I asked. My mouth was suddenly dry, and I thought, I can't be thinking this.

He stared straight ahead.

"Will they look like us—in your dream?"

"I'm not sure of that part," he said. "Life would have to be carbon-based, even there. I did try to draw them once."

"Oh?"

"I threw it out. I thought that maybe—you know, when you draw, another part of your mind could come out, like when you sleep. But I can't draw, I can't do . . . things like that so well. My fingers haven't caught up. It came out looking stupid, like little green men or something. And it isn't like that," he said calmly. "But circles, I think they will have circles. To offset the effects of their mass increase."

"What will they do," I said, "after they know we're intelligent? After they meet one of us?"

He leaned back against the head of his bed. "I don't know," he said, and he looked sad for an instant. "I keep waking up."

FOURTEEN

1 had a lot of thinking to do and I couldn't do it in my house. In my room I kept looking out at Harold's driveway and yard; I must have seen Mrs. Miller go out about three times and check her mailbox before she finally retrieved a big stack of envelopes she stuffed into her plaid pocket. I lined up my books of pennies, but all I could think of when I saw Lincoln's head repeated over and over again was how he had a nickname for being honest. I went out and sat by Chief's house for a while; he seemed glad to see me and then less so when he realized I hadn't brought him anything extra to eat. He wasn't really limping that much anymore, not enough to get me mad all over again.

Later that afternoon I set off, across the street. I went back through the grass and weeds, and the ground was mushy under my feet.

There were lots of birds in the trees, chirping and having a great time, a party really, now that it was spring for good.

I found a place in the woods where a tree had fallen over. It wasn't a thick tree, and it was still connected by a strip of wood to its trunk, so it shifted a little this way and that as I sat on it.

I lifted my legs in the air and tried to balance, but had to keep touching my feet down to the ground to steady myself. Once I almost tipped over backward and felt a moment of panic.

I knew I could get up and walk to my right, which would be north, which, even though I couldn't see it, was in the direction of the constellation Andromeda, and its star Alpheratz—and continue on, toward the constellation Ursa Major, and come upon Harold's house, and then maybe I could show the jerk how to swing a bat properly. Or just at this instant in the universe—where somewhere there was a star exploding, somewhere a nova—I could stand up and walk left, in the direction of Rigel, the brightest star in Orion's belt, and even, as a kind of ultimate betrayal, toward the place where Sirius, Sothis, was fixed in the sky—and I could come upon the shack and give a yell like the hunter Orion gave when the scorpion stung him and he ascended into the heavens. I could give a yell like his own dog must have given when he saw that he had failed to protect his master—and when they opened the door I could tell Keith and Robby and Jim—especially Jim—all that Harold had told me.

And this time they would listen. I knew I would be able to make them listen.

I tried to balance a couple more times on the tree. Then I started walking in the direction of Sirius.

———

I waited outside the shack. They had added something new to it, beams they must have stolen from the house sometime after we'd raided it, now nailed into the plywood like columns.

The door was yanked open, and a nail threatened to pop out of one of the hinges.

"It's you-know-who," said Robby, and withdrew his head into the shack.

Keith appeared in the doorway. "Yeah?"

"I've got something to tell you."

"What about?"

"Harold."

I heard someone say something from inside. "Yeah," Keith said to him, and then to me, "I thought you knew, we're all finished with that."

He started to close the door.

"Was that Jim?" I asked.

"Jim's not here yet," said Keith.

"He'll want to hear," I said. "No matter what you think."

"Then what is it?"

"Only when Jim's here."

Keith muttered something into the shack. Then to me: "Wait if you want. It's a free country." He started to close the door.

"Out here?"

He paused a moment, considering. Then he let the door hang open, and went inside.

I glanced around—just woods on all sides, buds popping from the branches—and I walked through the door.

They were playing cards. Robby was sitting on a stump and Keith on the old kitchen chair. A piece was

106

now missing from its back. The crate was between them, and each had stacks of pennies they were betting. I thought about looking through the coins . . . and then it seemed that was a little kid's idea. I leaned against a wall and watched. It was April, and there was a new girl on their calendar. She didn't look much older than a high-school girl.

Robby was dealing from a set of Bicycle cards. "How many?" he asked Keith.

"Two."

"Dealer takes three."

Keith put a stack of pennies in the center of the crate, and said without looking at me, "This better be good, Donald."

"It is," I said. I thought it sounded close to the cool, flattened way they were talking.

"I'll see you and raise you five," said Robby. He put in a taller stack of pennies.

Keith put in five more pennies, and they looked at each other without expression. Poker faces.

"Two pairs, jacks over eights," said Keith.

"Three little ladies," said Robby, slowly fanning his cards.

"Damn," said Keith, throwing his cards down, while Robby scooped the coins toward him, some of which fell through the spaces between the boards of the crate.

I realized suddenly they were trying to act and talk like gamblers you'd see on detective shows or Westerns.

They played another game, and Robby won again, and this time when he brought the coins toward him, he said, "Come to Papa." Then he brought his hand up quickly to his mouth and sucked it. He'd gotten a

107

splinter in the fleshy edge of his hand, and Keith laughed.

Keith had dealt out three cards for the next game when Jim opened the door.

He nodded at them, and then raised his eyebrows at me.

"I found out some stuff," I said.

Jim smiled as he walked toward the car seat. "One thing you got to say about this guy, he doesn't give up. So," he said to me, "is it good?"

"It's a royal flush," I said.

Jim laughed, but Robby looked unsure.

"Tell him," said Jim.

"In poker," I said, "it's the best hand."

When I finished, nobody said anything for a while. Then Keith said, "It's too weird."

Robby shifted his gaze from Keith to Jim, who was sitting a little ways from the crate. He glanced at me, and back at Jim. "I kind of like it," said Robby. "Wait, I know. We get a big plate—like a pie plate, only bigger. We paint it silver and some night when he's sitting out on his back steps we sail it toward him and make weird noises. It'll scare the hell out of him."

Jim moved his head once, side to side. All the time I'd been telling it, he had been quiet and seemed to be thinking things over. Now he said to Robby, even as he looked at me, "You're on the right track, but that's the Classic Comics version." I knew he understood, and I felt I'd crossed a line, as I had when Harold first started to talk to me about his dream.

"So what's this about Saturdays?" asked Keith.

"I don't know. They all go off somewhere."

"So how will we ever get him alone, if we did decide to try something?" Keith had a disgusted look on his face.

"Well—" I began.

Keith stood up suddenly. "How do we know he's not playing a trick on us? Doing some experiment to us? To teach us some kind of lesson or something." He walked in a tight circle. "And even if we could do it, if the time worked out, it's too crazy." He looked at Jim. "No matter what some people have been saying. So he had this dream, lots of people have dreams. He'd never fall for it, he wouldn't believe it."

Jim raised his eyebrows.

"You know, maybe not," Robby said to Keith. "But maybe he would. Let's say you had some dream that you're really not that good, you're not that interested in sports. But you try so hard because your father would kill you if you didn't. So now you hate them, you really hate them. And somehow somebody knew that, and showed you they knew. You'd sure be bothered by that."

"What are you—" said Keith, as Jim whistled.

"It's the same with Harold," I interrupted. "Maybe he won't buy it—but if he doesn't that's okay, he'll still see that we know, that I told all of you. He'll feel like a fool. Disgraced, kind of. And then, just maybe, he will buy it," I said. "At least for a while, even for a minute or two, if we come up with something right enough. And that would be worth everything."

Keith's face was red; he was looking from one to the other of us.

"We can just see how far we can get him to go with it," said Jim. "And at any point, if it falls through, it will still be good. Like Donald says. And then our idea, of getting back at somebody this way, we would have proved it, that it could be done. Like a new weapon."

"Better than an arrow," said Robby.

"But what's this about me?" Keith said to Robby, his face still flushed.

"I was just—"

"Cool down," said Jim. "He was just trying to make you understand. Everybody knows if you strike out once your old man won't let you forget it for a week."

"Well," Keith said to Robby, and then he seemed to think of something. "At least my old man knows *which* kid's football game he's coming to see."

"Hey," said Jim.

"With his beer can in his little paper bag. And I won't even start with you," he said to Jim.

"Hey," said Jim, sharper.

Keith and Robby had lowered their eyes. Robby was biting his hand where he'd gotten the splinter. I remembered how Harold had bitten his knuckle that day in his room. Something had gone out of Keith's face, and it looked slack, like a little kid's pudgy face.

Jim was bobbing his head, as if everything was fine, but there was that vein in his forehead again.

After a moment, he spoke: "So you said right before or after that star . . . Sirius . . . leaves. Where is it now?"

"It set," I said. Robby and Keith stared at me blankly. "Because of the earth's position."

Jim was quiet again, thinking.

"Remember that Halloween stunt Gillespie did?" Keith said suddenly.

"The nun?" asked Robby.

"The year before."

"The Creature from the Lark Dagoon, he called it," said Robby, and Keith and he nodded at each other.

"Headless," said Jim. "But you could put something there."

"Masks," I said. I faced Keith. "And then he'd never know who it was."

"Is he nearsighted or farsighted?" Jim asked.

"I'm not sure."

"Farsighted is when the eyes look all funny through their glasses. Nearsighted, they don't," said Robby. I closed my eyes and pictured Harold, as I heard Robby say, "My one brother—"

"He's nearsighted," I said.

"Good," said Jim. "He can't see far away."

"Listen," said Keith. "If his parents ever find out . . . You know his father's got a bad temper, he . . . he blew his top with some juniors who were bugging him to get a test drive."

"We'll have to be certain they're not home," said Jim, and smiled to himself. I didn't know how he could make sure, but I didn't want to ask.

"So we'll do it?" said Jim.

Still I looked down for a moment, until I saw how it could all make sense. That it wasn't such a bad thing, maybe, to give the poor boy what he wanted.

When I lifted my head, the others were nodding at Jim.

FIFTEEN

The next Saturday was clear and the Buick stayed in Harold's driveway all day. Jim had said that whether the Buick was there or not was very crucial to our plans, but he didn't explain further. He just said he'd done some scouting around. During our couple of meetings in the shack, we'd finished most of the work on the inside of the structure, and stashed what else we needed there. And we thought up excuses to tell our parents why we were going to be getting up at the crack of dawn on a Saturday, and disappearing for the rest of the day.

I prepared my parents by informing them there was a paper drive for the science club at school, and my mother said that was nice, that it seemed like a worthwhile thing to do. On the day the Buick remained in the driveway, I had to explain why it was called off.

"Because the driver got sick," I said. She was looking through her pattern book.

"You know. The driver of the truck. To put the papers in."

"Of course," said my mother. I had the feeling I could have told her what we were really up to and she wouldn't really hear it, she'd just say it was all fine. She brushed her hair away from her forehead, and then glanced at me.

"But he'll get better soon," I said. "You don't need to worry about that."

During that week, and the week following, Harold only rode the bus twice, and I stayed after school a couple of days just so I wouldn't have to ride home with him. I didn't want to talk about far-off planets, and it seemed as if he didn't, either. It was as if he'd gotten something out of his system and didn't need to talk about it now. One day, he complained that Mrs. Saunders was giving him too much homework. I had to look at him twice, because it was something a normal kid would say.

But I wasn't feeling too normal with him myself. During our few walks home together I was either silent or gabbing about anything but stars, dogs, and aliens. When we passed by the now-finished house one afternoon there was a parked car and a family walking around the lot—a man and a woman and two small kids who must have been their son and daughter. The kids seemed excited and the father and mother were laughing as the kids ran up to the front door and peeked in through its glass.

"They can see the living room," I said to Harold. "Isn't it funny how people say that, as if the room was alive, like it was made up of trees or plants?" He didn't say anything. "It would be something if you could really have a room like that, and the thing about it would be that whenever someone in the family

113

walked into it—no matter what kind of tough day they'd had—they'd come alive. They'd be alive and you'd be alive and you'd be together in that room, with the living trees for walls . . ."

I shut up then, because I saw him looking back at the house.

The father had a key and he was opening the door and the kids were starting to run inside.

"That house just looks like a stupid little box," he said, squinting through his glasses. Out of nowhere I felt suddenly glad again for what we were planning.

Later in the second week, my father said he wanted to clear out his mind, so he took me and Chief to the park. Chief jumped out of the car when we arrived; he looked happy to be there again. My father and I stood by the car and waited for him to go running around like he used to. But he'd gotten fat and lazy since he'd been hurt, and he acted like his paw caused him more pain than I thought it probably did. He loped around for a little while as my father and I watched. Then he came over to us, and walked in a little circle, and lay down with his head on his paws.

"We've got to stop feeding him so much," said my father.

"Yeah," I said, but somehow I knew we wouldn't.

He had a little trouble jumping back up into the car. I had to help him with his hind legs, and when I pushed him up he turned and snapped at me, and I felt my eyes smarting for no reason I could think of.

The second Saturday was almost too perfect. A little before six in the morning, I heard a car start and I put my face to the window. It was foggy, but there wasn't any drizzle. A ghostly shape, like the soul of a 1956 Buick, drifted backward out of Harold's driveway. Two points of red light flicked on, a horn tooted once, softly, and then the fog swallowed it all up, the way a dream fades when you wake.

I thought how they wouldn't have tooted if no one was home.

Out in the kitchen, I dialed Jim's number. It rang for a split second, and then stopped. He'd picked it up and without saying anything had put it down, for I heard the dial tone come back on. He'd gotten my signal; now he would call Keith, who would in turn call Robby, all of them waiting by the phone to grab it off its cradle the first moment it rang, so if their parents heard it at all it wouldn't sound real, just a night sound in a dream.

I didn't know if my parents had woken up or not. I supposed my father had, that he had learned in the army to come alert at the slightest sound that might spell danger. I dressed quickly and walked out the front door and down the stairs. I heard a faint bark from the back yard, and then I continued down the driveway, and if anybody was watching me from the window, they would have seen me disappear into the fog.

They'll come by and pick us up on the street, I had told them, *a little after dawn.*

I kept my eyes on the ground. Everything was colorless from the mist, the asphalt driveway, the perfect grass. I jumped backward when I got to the road in front of our house: two burning torches were bearing

115

down on me, smoking wildly. Then a car shushed by—it was only headlights in the fog. I could see it was Mr. Roscoe from down the block in his old Dodge, returning from the night shift at Republic Steel.

I made it fine past the house across the street, but I knew it would get harder once I left that back yard. I was right: I could still see the ground, but tree limbs came at me suddenly out of the mist, and I had to duck and raise my hands as if avoiding a blow.

I heard the rushing water in the ravine. I carefully started over the side, and although I skidded a little, this time I didn't fall. At the bottom, the mist was curling off the water like smoke.

I wandered around some on the far side of the gully—the fog was thicker here. Then I heard voices and laughter, and went more to my left.

I walked right in without knocking. Jim and Robby were still in their regular clothes. Although the mist hadn't penetrated the walls, it was dark inside. I could just make out the charts, and the yokes of wood with the cloth hanging down, lined up one, two, three. The spray paint on the balls seemed to be holding. The portable radio was on the crate, out of sight of the auto seat now bolted to some planks. Even though I knew what everything was, it was a pretty good effect—I only hoped it would be good enough. I walked over to the window and pushed a little against the black cloth there, with the holes I'd pricked in, some big, some small. You could make out Orion. Gemini. I turned and squinted my eyes until everything in the shack was blurry: the effect was better.

Jim handed me the camera. "It's just this button," he said.

I took it, feeling its weight in my hands.

"Try and be careful with it," he said. "It was my dad's."

"Did you see Keith?" asked Robby.

I shook my head. Jim looked grim. "We all agreed," he said.

I walked over and looked out the door of the shack. "The fog's a good thing," I said. "It isn't lifting."

"Not yet," said Jim. Then he cursed.

I started to close the door and Keith rushed in, and I was pushed back, against the part of the room we'd fixed up. Some silver paper tore.

"Watch what you're doing!" said Jim. He was speaking to Keith.

"He's the one—" said Keith, but Jim put up his hand. He walked over to where the paper tore and inspected it.

"Yeah, that'll really fool him," said Keith.

"Take it down—no, put up another sheet over it," Jim said to Robby. Then he turned to Keith: "It will when he has his glasses off."

"You're late," said Robby.

Keith shrugged. "I almost couldn't get out. They got up when I did. They'd never heard of a baseball practice in the fog."

"That's what you told them?" asked Jim.

"My mother knows the other mothers; she'd never buy the class trip."

"Well, they can just call up the coach," said Jim quietly.

"I told them it wasn't with Coach. Just a bunch of us guys. An extra practice. Before the season starts."

"In the fog?"

"That's what my mother said, when she saw how it was out. But I said it would make it harder. A ball would come right at you—you'd only have a split second to react. Like a line drive coming toward the mound. I was making it up as I went along, but you-know-who bought it. I think he liked it."

Jim shook his head, smiling a little. "Maybe you're not as dumb as you look. Come on."

Keith walked over and put the yoke over Jim's shoulders. The black cloth hung over and hid him, all the way to the ground.

"It *is* pretty good," Keith said, taking a few steps back.

The costume was sitting on his shoulders a little crooked, and I helped him adjust it.

"Now for your head," I said. I brought over one of the balls, and let the cord we'd attached to it go down through the hole where the neck would be, so he could tie it under his chin. I felt like a dad helping a Little Leaguer with his baseball cap.

"Can you see all right?" There was a little tear you could hardly find in the creature's chest.

"Yep," he said after a moment.

Keith and Robby grabbed their yokes and silvery spheres, and we left the shack and started out through the fog.

I walked ahead, and they followed. I wasn't dressed up, so I could move more easily. I could hear them stumbling and cursing behind me, and Keith shouted out, "Hey, will you slow down!" which made me smile to myself. Keith and Robby were carrying the balls under their arms, but Jim had kept his on: he was probably trying to get the moves right.

We walked through the woods, behind the houses, behind where the lawns ended, with their little fountains and trelliswork and patios, the hooded grills and lawn chairs that were set in circles; we traipsed through the brambles and low-hanging branches we could hardly see in the mist, and they tore at our clothes and scratched off silver bits of paint like the blood of an alien race.

Halfway to Harold's house, I turned around and watched them struggle up to me.

"This is good!" I said. I suddenly felt so happy to be there with them on this crazy stunt.

"What?" asked Jim. "What'd he say?" He couldn't hear too well through the suit around him.

"Nothing," I said, and laughed. "Let's go!"

When we got to the thin woods behind Harold's house, they waited in the trees and I walked forward with the camera. I hadn't taken more than about eight steps when the fog swallowed them up. I strode back quickly to where they were waiting. Keith and Robby were struggling to put on their heads.

"You'll have to come up closer," I said. "He'll never see you if you stay back there. Just until you can see the outline of his house—stop there. Watch for the signal."

Keith mumbled something, but I didn't wait to hear. I started forward again through the fog, in a crouch.

I made my way through the back yard, under the metal T of a clothesline pole, until I reached his house. There was the bat and ball lying on the ground. I cut left, keeping alongside the house, but out of sight of any windows. Then I thought, if he wasn't home, or his parents were, none of these precautions would keep me from the trouble I'd be in.

I walked around the corner, and stopped.

Ahead of me was his window, where I'd first come upon the telescope. But with the fog swirling around it, it looked like a window back through time. I waited a moment—I had an unbearable feeling of excitement. I crept forward and tapped sharply on it, where the curtains were closed.

I tried to control my breathing as I waited under the window a little to the side. I had remembered from being inside his room that you couldn't see where I was now, because the telescope was in the way; you could only see out in the other direction. I put the camera against the glass. Then I reached up and tapped once more, gently.

I counted to ten, and then to ten again, thinking he had gone away, that Jim had been wrong, when the curtain did start to move. Right when it opened, I hit the button of the camera and the flashbulb ignited. I hoped it had gone off right in his eyes—and that he wouldn't be able to tell if it was close or far, a meteor just outside the glass or the far-off light wave of a ship. I popped the bulb onto the grass, where it sizzled. Then I ran in a crouch alongside the house, turning the corner back to the way I'd come. I clicked in a second bulb and made another flash by the back window to draw him out of his room. The second flash was the signal. I clicked in a third, and when the back curtain started to move slowly aside, I let it off. Then I scooted along the base of his house, back toward the side where his window was, and waited.

After a moment I looked around the corner, into the back yard, and I caught my breath.

Three strange figures were now just visible in the swirling mist. They appeared to be gliding over the ground, wearing filmy black suits, with large round heads that had neither eyes nor ears nor mouths—just silver circles, really—that could grow and diminish without harm, after they'd reached the full speed of light outside the pull of Sirius.

When I heard the back door rattle, I drew my head in a little. The back door opened, the creatures halted—and Harold walked out onto his back porch, blinking, trying to stare through the sunbursts of flash that must still be in his eyes.

SIXTEEN

Harold stood on the porch, rubbing his eyes, squinting as if he was trying to make out the figures. I had always thought this would be the time that he might laugh, or look at the Halloween-like creatures we were trying to fool him with and say, "Come on, you guys." But as I watched the scene before me unfold I saw why he didn't do either of those things. You couldn't see the figures distinctly, they seemed to be shapes emerging from smoke, perhaps burning with a flameless fire. Harold shook once, all over, and reached back for the doorknob, and I had the feeling, maybe shared with him in that moment, that these weren't my friends, that he was really meeting beings from another world on some planetary landscape with shifting shapes and clouds of chemicals blowing by.

He took a step down the first stair, still rubbing the flash from his eyes. From what I could see of his face, he looked terrified, and he hesitated there. Jim and I had talked about how when you're little you wait for Santa Claus with the milk and the cookies, but if you ever happened to really see him . . . and what if he didn't look like jolly Kris Kringle but like some tall being hundreds of years old, dressed in dark red, not even human, with distant, powerful eyes that had seen your parents, and their parents before them and their parents in turn, all the way back in time . . . Harold glanced back at the house and took another step. They were about four yards from him, still half hidden by the fog. The flash must be clearing from his eyes, they didn't have much time before they tried the next thing . . .

He put his foot into space, and then down onto the next and final concrete stair. Still they stood there and gazed at him from their eyeless faces. I couldn't figure out why they didn't do what we had planned, and then tried to console myself that even if it all fell apart now, if Harold cried out that they wouldn't really look like that, or started giggling, it was still a success and we could still talk about it in the halls. *Why didn't they move?* And then I saw why they didn't.

Harold was moving. Or at least his hand was.

From the pocket of his pajamas, he was carefully, as if he'd rehearsed it, bringing out a folded brown paper bag.

Then he offered them a cookie.

You could tell the creatures didn't know what to do at first. Perhaps they hadn't expected this sign of friendship from an earthling. Finally Keith—it was hard to distinguish between him and Robby, who were both standing a little to the front of Jim—glided for-

ward, and took it in the thick rubber plumber's glove
he'd gotten from Robby's father's truck. His strange
head—the beach ball we'd spray-painted silver—wobbled a little back and forth as he moved. To Harold it
must have seemed as if the creature was nodding.

*They would have known that was a way to show friend-
ship; they would have studied it through their telescopes.*

Despite the uncanniness of the scene, I expected it to
be over now. He'd gotten a pretty good look at them.

And perhaps it would have been if Keith hadn't
done what he did next.

He dropped the cookie to the ground as if it meant
nothing.

Harold watched it land on the grass, a little brown
spot. Then he brought his hand up to his mouth, and I
saw that he was biting his knuckle, chewing away on
it, thinking, or perhaps trying to show them what to
do with the cookie.

And before they could do the thing they were supposed to do next, he did it for them. He took off his
glasses.

He held them away from his head, and tapped on
the frames and on the lenses.

*They would want to know if someone was wearing some-
thing manufactured, metal or glass.*

Harold folded the arms of the glasses and opened
them up again; he put them on and took them off.

And then Robby did the exactly right thing: he took
two steps forward and put out his gloved hand. But I
did a double-take and decided we should pack it in.
He'd done the right thing, but the wrong way: he was
wearing a pink rubber glove he must have swiped

from his mother. I didn't know why he had that on; maybe his father would mix up his sons but make no mistake over how many gloves he kept in his toolbox. And why had he given the good one to Keith and kept this for himself? But Harold didn't seem to mind. He handed his glasses forward. And I had to admit, the flash of pink—almost fleshlike—was eerily right coming from the seven-foot black-robed creature with the silver sphere for a head and its arms sticking out from where its hips should be.

Robby couldn't exactly see what he was doing with the pair of small black glasses—the peepholes were in the middle part of the creature's chest, and anything above that was outside his perspective. He brought them too close, actually right into the ball, which pushed it back a little. It looked like some combination of seeing, eating, and smelling, and I thought that luck was again on our side: he wasn't holding them up to the sky or trying them on, the way you'd expect someone from Earth to handle a pair of glasses.

The creature turned and showed the spectacles to the creature next to him. He seemed to regard them— again his silvery head bobbed. The creature then showed the glasses to the creature behind. Now they were all nodding at the glasses. It reminded me of a film I'd seen in geography class, of a bunch of Stone Age natives handing around a metal knife.

Finally they finished with the glasses, and the first creature took them inside his robe, and I found myself thinking, *He's putting them in a specimen pouch.*

Harold was watching them, squinting. When his glasses disappeared, his shoulders slumped. You could almost feel how much he hated to give them up, how the creatures would stay ghosts now, just out of the range of his vision. And everything else he would miss.

The four of them stood there. Harold appeared younger without his spectacles, and once again terrified. You wait for Santa Claus but if you ever happened to really see him, and look into his ageless eyes . . .

After a moment, Harold started moving his hands. Together and apart, together and apart, again in a patterned, practiced way. Three fingers, then what looked like a clenched fist, then a V-for-victory sign, then a cupped half circle, and other motions I couldn't make out as he moved, showing each of the signals in turn. What was he doing? Then I recognized them. Letters. From the chart on his wall. Again and again. He was spelling out a word in the fog, in the International Language of the Deaf.

Finally, the creature in the rear raised his hand. Harold took what seemed to be an involuntary step back, squinting at him. The being took a step forward, and when Harold saw his raised hand, he dropped his own. The being was signaling: Stop.

They would have known what that meant; they would have studied it through their telescopes.

The two near creatures walked up to either side of Harold. One put his hand lightly on Harold's shoulder—Harold slumped a little and then stood straight again. They turned him around so he was facing back toward his house.

The front of his pajamas was wet.

The two creatures spread out a long black cloth between them; then they gently put it over his eyes. Harold slumped again, but remained standing. They turned him back around. I thought it was going further than we'd had any right to expect it would, and I wasn't sure why. And what they were doing now reminded me of getting someone ready for a firing squad.

We hadn't figured out how to direct him to the shack. Keith and Robby went ahead with him, and tried pushing him for a while with the flat of their gloved hands. Sometimes they just let him wander into a tree, and then you could see Harold flailing his arms at the limbs as if they were attacking him. Then when he'd get back into the clear, he'd start saying something to them, in a patient voice.

Finally, Jim motioned Keith to come back for a moment and let Robby walk ahead with Harold.

"Lead him by the hand," Jim whispered.

"What?" Keith's voice was muffled and his hearing must have been, too, underneath the cloth.

"Take him by the hand, we want to get him to the shack in one piece."

"You think I'm some fairy? Have Donald do it."

"Then tell Robby to!"

Keith started to turn, when Jim asked him, "What's he saying?"

"He's saying we couldn't possibly know but the trees could hurt him."

"He's not so scared if he's talking, then."

"He peed his pants," said Keith, and crashed ahead through the thin woods.

I stood there a moment with the tall silver-headed

127

creature in the rising trails of mist. I told myself that if you saw he wouldn't hurt you, you might be able to feel safe. But now the creature seemed to be suffering shoulder tremors, perhaps a sign of threatening behavior, or of some grave biochemical shutdown here in the earth's atmosphere. The creature's head lifted off—I caught my breath for a moment—and then the cape moved aside and I could see Jim's face in the folds of cloth. I laughed for a second, with relief.

"He's really going for it," I said.

"He is," said Jim, grinning but tense.

"Maybe he'll stop being scared," I said.

"Maybe." He was quiet for a moment. Then he started to put his head back on, but I touched his arm to stop him. I wanted to talk to him some more, before he became a creature again.

"We'll have to see how far it goes," I said.

He looked at me. "Just hope it doesn't go too far."

"What do you mean?"

"Just something I learned: the barn always goes up." Then he tied on the strings, the head rocked forward on the yoke, and I was looking once again at a face without expression.

We walked up to join Keith. Ahead, Harold was holding on to Robby's pink Playtex glove like a little kid holding on to the hand of his mother, walking down the dark hall toward his room. Still in his pajamas, filled with trust.

Robby pulled him along the path ahead of us, but once in a while I could see him lead him too close to a stump; with no branches to warn him, Harold would stumble, and once he fell flat on his stomach. I saw the shoulders of Keith's creature shaking as he tried to control his laughter.

"I'm okay," said Harold, as he got up. There was dirt along the front of his pajamas with their little pattern of sailboats. "I'm not sure you can understand me—but you shouldn't . . . The stumps can hurt me, too."

I saw Keith bring his glove into his mouth. He was biting it now so he wouldn't laugh out loud. The whole body of the tall creature was shaking, head wobbling, with its claw inside its chest.

Finally we got in sight of the shack. The fog was lifting, and the trees around were more distinct and colorful. Above us, there were patches of blue and white, and sunshine burning through. When we were about twenty yards away, Keith's head dropped off. I imagined a man in a lab coat with a pointer at a chart, saying, "It was the effects of the oxygen-rich atmosphere . . ." Keith walked a ways before he knew it, and then turned around and saw it lying on the ground.

He ran toward it, almost tripping over his cape, and then picked it up and mimicked doing broken-field running with a football toward the door of the shack.

Jim's creature took a step forward and stopped, and I knew that under his getup he was tense with anger. These kinds of high jinks could ruin the whole thing. Now Keith was walking back, and he seemed to understand the true meaning of Harold's blindfold, for he did a kind of mocking dance in front of him, putting his thumb on his real nose and wiggling his fingers in his glove.

"What is it?" asked Harold. He looked frightened again. "What's there?"

Keith made a dirty gesture at Harold and then motioned over to me. I walked up to him and started to help him fasten his head back on. Then I put my mouth right by the hole where his eyes were and said as softly as I could, "Jim wants you to cut it out."

Keith brought up his hand and punched me under the ribs, and it was all I could do not to cough.

Before I knew what I was doing, I smacked Keith where I thought his nose would be, a good, flat-handed hit—and then Jim stepped up between us, put a hand on each of our shoulders, and gripped us hard. He shook us both a little and then he stepped back.

Keith took a stride toward me, with his glove balled into a fist, and I dropped back. Now I was in some kind of trouble with Keith, and I could only hope that he'd somehow forget about it before it was all over. I told myself that I had lost my head for a moment, feeling I wouldn't let any alien from some far-off planetary system push me around. In fact, I think I had been waiting to do something like that for a while.

"What's happening?" asked Harold. "Can you understand me? Are there four of you or three?"

That more than anything stopped us. I felt crummy all of a sudden—it made me think how I was as much a part of what was going on as the others, when for a while I'd been pretending I had just come upon this strange happening in the woods.

I walked ahead then—giving a wide berth to Keith—and went into the shack as we'd planned if it went this far. I couldn't understand, if he was so smart, why it was working to this extent.

I paused for a moment inside the doorway—you could hear the sound of spring in Ohio all around us—crickets, birds, insects buzzing. Life may be carbon-based in other parts of the universe, but it wouldn't sound exactly like this, nor would these sounds penetrate any kind of spacecraft that could fly farther than Akron. I turned on the portable radio low—it was playing some song about teenagers in love—and then I moved the dial, until I got both static and a kind of high-pitched whining sound.

When they led him in the door and closed it behind him, I turned the volume up high. The electronic sounds muffled out the birds and bugs.

They half pushed and half led him to the seat bolted to the planks, and I thought how it fit that this whole thing began and was ending with him in a car seat. Keith and Robby brought out their belts—the same belts they wore to school, perhaps, now spray-painted silver.

"What are you doing?" Harold asked.

They looped the belts around him and strapped him tightly to the chair. His hands and arms were moving futilely; he couldn't get his fingers to touch, but I could see he was trying to spell out the same word he had in his yard, three fingers, a clenched fist, a V-for-victory sign . . .

Jim pointed at the radio. I turned the volume up higher so the static came on really loud, right behind Harold. Robby and Keith went into action. They carefully picked up the boards the seat was bolted to, so

Harold would only have the slightest sensation of floating off the ground. Then they lifted first one side and then the other—Harold cried out—and they rocked the chair side to side in midair, a baby's cradle in the sky. Then Robby, who was in the back, knelt down, and Keith lifted the ends of the front two boards. Harold was now tilting upward. We'd all tried it the week before—sitting in the chair with my eyes closed, I'd had moments of feeling as if the shack was rocketing to the moon.

I lowered the volume, and Jim and I each grabbed a side of the car seat. The other two put a length of red carpet they'd filched from somewhere over the boards, and then we all carefully lowered Harold to the floor of the shack.

"Can't I see?" he was saying. "Won't you let me see?" He paused and seemed to think of something. "I won't tell. I won't hurt you."

Jim nodded to me. I brought the camera right up against his blindfold and let off another flash. He yelled and jerked his head back, which almost made me drop the camera. I didn't think it would scare him that much.

"You won't hurt me," he said in a shaky voice. "I always knew you wouldn't."

Robby reached around behind his head and took off the blindfold.

Harold sat there in the chair, blinking. The flash was still in his eyes and his glasses were off, but I had an idea what he was seeing. I squinted my eyes to get the effect: everything silver around him, with a red floor of some kind under his feet. A dim interior—outside the window, the darkness of space with the pinpoint light of distant stars. Three strange creatures in a tri-angle-like pyramid before him, and the high whining sound of space all around. On the wall ahead, he might be able to make out a chart as the explosion cleared from his eyes: it was a map, represented not by shapes but by rows of numbers. On the floor by the rear creature, there was a live cricket in a glass case, a second specimen from the planet. He wouldn't be able to turn his head enough to see the rest of the ship extending behind him, the long silver hallways, the other creatures working at charts and laboratory tables, like a colony of praying mantises . . .

"Oh, my God," he said. "I am still dreaming—I'm in my dream. I didn't think you'd look . . . I can't believe this." He squinted at the silver globes of the aliens. "Where are your eyes? Are you like . . . insects . . . your whole head a huge eye . . . ?"

He squinted at the little glass case on the ground. "Is that why you have the . . . insect? Do you speak?"

He looked at them and they stood silently, as if star-ing back. In the dim light the silvery globes really looked metallic, as if they'd changed. It was odd, I felt there *was* space all around us, that we really were float-ing there, and all our houses and families were just specks of dust on the planet below . . .

"If I am dreaming," he said, and then he broke off. "There's so much I want to ask." His eyes lit on them one by one, and then settled on Jim, at the apex of the pyramid.

"You're the leader?"

We hadn't really planned on what we were going to

do next. They could all just take off their costumes and it would be a wonderful joke here, something Harold would never live down when it got out in the neighborhood and school. It was one of those stunts that would live forever. "Remember when those guys were spacemen and fooled that smart kid—yeah, it was Keith and Jim and Donald and someone else"—the three of us linked together forever in legend, especially Jim and me, the brains behind it. It was a feat that would make a burning arrow in a barn door, scaring someone with a snake, seem foolish. "Yeah, he messed up Donald's dog—and Donald, he doesn't like to be messed with—"

But I don't think any of us wanted to stop here. I knew I was wondering how much further we could take it, how much more we could find out.

"There's so much I want to know," Harold said. He tried to bring his hands together again—then gave up and settled back in his chair.

The cricket chirped. "It's a cricket," said Harold. "*Orthoptera Gryllidae.*"

Suddenly there was a voice in response, as if the cricket had answered. I jumped and Harold jerked his head up. The voice seemed to be coming from the midst of the creatures, as if from the three of them, from some force field they made in their triangle, for the silvery globes hadn't moved or registered a change. The voice was coming from underneath one of the capes, of course—Jim's—but he made his voice sound strange, thin and high like silver wire, and stopping after each word, as if he'd never start up again.

"*You . . . . . don't ask . . . . . We . . . . . ask.*"

"You speak English!" Harold said excitedly. "One, two, three, four," he said. "One, two, four, eight, sixteen," he continued rapidly. "Two, four, sixteen, two hundred fifty-six. Two, eight, five hundred and twelve."

The creature nodded. Harold went on. "The cricket . . . the Ortho . . . is an insect. I'm a boy. Human being. *Homo sapiens.* I go to school. Live in a house. With parents. Woman and man." He was trying to imitate the way the creature spoke. "I . . . have . . . friends."

"Friends," the creature said, pronouncing it strangely, as if he had just learned it.

"Well, one," said Harold. "Another boy . . . Donald . . ."

The creature didn't say anything for a moment.

"And you," said Harold. "You're from . . . far . . . away?"

"We ask," said Jim, forgetting to hesitate.

"From Sirius?" asked Harold softly.

The creature remained silent.

"Sothis," whispered Harold.

Again, there was just the stillness of space, filled with the static.

"Are we going there?" asked Harold. The creature just stood before him, as if staring at him, expressionless.

"I know I'd be the . . . first person . . . I know it would take a while. Even at the speed of light. But maybe you've conquered that. How fast do you go?"

"Ninety-five miles an hour!" said Robby suddenly, trying to make his voice sound low—but it cracked in the middle of the phrase.

Harold's face was screwed up in thought. "It must

be a different system. Maybe you mean, to me, really really fast."

The first creature nodded.

"Would . . . I be . . . the first to visit?" He smiled a little—bravely, I thought. "Me and the cricket. That would be really something . . . for you, too. You could ask questions of me, and I . . . would ask . . . questions of you. I wouldn't, you know, be any trouble. Bother. Just for a while I'd visit. I can see the sizes of your brains must be so much greater than mine. Their capacity. What I knew or how I was wouldn't really seem like anything . . . nothing strange. I mean . . . all your kids, um, offspring, probably would be . . . like that. In your silver cities." He looked terrifically sad for a moment. "In your shining cities . . ."

The whine on the radio shifted, and I adjusted the dial. I must have turned it the wrong way, toward the frequency of a station, for a disc jockey's voice came on, saying it was fifty-nine degrees and mostly sunny. I rotated it the other way quickly, and the static and high-pitched whine resumed.

"That's how you learn to speak," Harold said suddenly. "You monitor Earth's broadcasts!"

The three creatures as one dipped their round silvery orbs slightly.

"I knew it," said Harold.

Even our mistakes were fooling him—ninety-five miles per hour, weather reports on the radio—were we really that good? And then it struck me why—for whatever reason, he wanted so badly to believe.

Now Keith turned and walked back to the cricket cage. He reached down on the floor next to it and

136

picked up a small silver cup—he'd found it in his attic—and carried it toward Harold. I hadn't wanted him to do this, but he had insisted, and it seemed we had to let him if we wanted him to go along.

He held the cup in front of Harold and let Harold peer down into it.

"What's this?"

"*Protection . . . . . from ship,*" said the creature in black.

Harold squinted around him. "I suppose, all the radiation," he said softly. "What do I do with it?"

The creature holding the cup produced a strange utensil. It was really a spoon that Keith had hammered flat. He brought the spoon to his silver globe of a head.

"You want me to . . . eat it . . . ingest it?"

The creature nodded.

"What is it?"

The creature nodded again, saying nothing.

Now Harold nodded. Keith put the silver oval of the utensil into the dark mixture, and brought it to Harold's mouth. It looked like he was feeding a baby. It was chocolate and mustard and ketchup with a little bit of dirt thrown in, and Keith had insisted on spitting in it once as he mixed it up.

After Harold swallowed it, a shudder passed over his face. I thought it would serve Keith right if he threw up all over him. But Harold nodded again. "It's . . . it's . . . okay."

Keith stepped away from him, backward.

Harold closed his eyes for a moment. "It's amazing how you do this," he said. "How you make it seem— like gravity. You know, the Earth's force. Even here. In this ship."

"*Orbit,*" said the creature in black.

"Yes," said Harold. He smiled a little—I thought once again he looked sad, not scared as I would have thought.

"Are we going there?"

"*You . . . . . want to . . . . . go?*" asked the leader.

Harold stared at him. "Yes."

"*But you . . . . . have . . . . . parents.*"

"Yes," said Harold, and looked down. He paused. "They won't—" he blurted out, and then caught himself. "I mean, today. They're gone today."

"*Gone,*" said the creature.

"They won't be back till . . . late." Harold took a breath and looked deep into the silver sphere of the creature, as if trying to find a face there. "There's this little place they go to . . . on a lake. You know, water. A body of water. Lake Erie." He squinted at the chart I'd typed full of numbers. "You probably have . . . the coordinates," he said. "A cottage. A small . . . house. We all go there, in the summers, when the earth is tilted to the sun . . . in the north . . . But they go there all year round . . . In the other seasons . . . No matter how the earth . . . My father—my male parent—he works so hard all week. He sells machines that drive. Like this ship—but on the land. Every now and then, every couple of weeks. You know, a week—seven days. One rotation of the earth, times seven. And then times three or four again. Every three or four, or five weeks. They go for the day. By themselves. The . . . two of them . . . and get back late. Sometimes the next morning . . . when the next rotation has already . . . started." He was biting his lip and he spoke very soft-

138

ly. "Still, I mind. Even though they need the time alone."

"*Why*," said the creature.

I shot a look at Jim, but Harold kept on.

"They're married," said Harold. "A custom we have. Man and woman. To be alone together, you see, until children . . . come along." He was biting his lip again, and the creature still stared at him like the blank face of the universe, a relentless force he couldn't escape. "One orbit around the sun, we call a year. Almost nine orbits, almost nine years ago, they were married. They never told me—I saw it." He was blinking, and I realized there were tears running down his cheeks. "Do you have schools? She had to . . . quit . . . school. I figured it out . . . with the math. You see, I was born . . . early . . ." He suddenly smiled up at the creature, as the cricket began to chirp. "I'm eight years old," he said, and looked down at where his arms were strapped in the belts. "Eight orbits. I can do the math. I'm very good at math."

Jesus Christ, I thought.

"*You're only eight years old?*" said the creature, forgetting to pause.

"At the end of this orbit I'll be nine," said Harold.

Jesus Christ, no wonder he looked so young and small. No wonder he believed this.

The creatures shifted uneasily on their feet. The leader banged his fist down on the cage and the cricket hopped and stopped chirping.

I thought back to the day when he held the golf club like a little kid—his father had been looking at his mother up in the window, and she wasn't crying at all.

They were looking at each other over his head—sharing a joke. Sharing a secret. Sharing a burden.

"So it is really okay if, if . . . I'm gone awhile." He stared at the creature in back. His face had taken on a determined look, the way I'd seen it that first day in the car. "I know, when you're quiet like that, you're communicating with one another."

The creature stared at him, hearing or not.

"Tell the others, it's . . . okay," said Harold. "Please."

The creature in back, the leader, walked past him. Then the other two followed. Harold looked after them as much as he could, but when his head was halfway turned, they were out of his line of vision. They walked out of the shack, ducking at the door, and I followed, quietly, so he wouldn't hear there was a fourth. I was still trying to pretend to myself the little details mattered.

We walked through the woods. It was a sunny day outside now, as the radio had predicted, and the contrast to the outer-space dimness of the inside of the shack made me blink. About thirty feet away, the first creature turned around and we all stopped.

"Jesus Christ," I heard Jim say, from the chest of the creature.

"Jerk," Keith said to me, and he reached to push me, but I stepped back.

"I didn't know," I said.

"You knew every other bloody, bloody thing."

"I can't believe it," said Robby.

"You could have known he was just a little kid," said Keith.

"He's so damn smart," said Robby.

140

"Cut it," said Jim. He was taking off his head, and then he laid it on the ground. The silver globe looked unworldly on the forest floor. Jim drew the front of his cloak apart, so I could see his face. "The thing is, now we just get him back."

I knew he was right, but I felt disappointed all the same.

"It was going pretty well," I said softly, wanting to believe it.

"Yeah, right," said Jim.

"Do we tell him?" asked Robby.

"No," said Jim. "If he doesn't know already—ninety-five miles an hour! We just hope he forgets it, I don't know, like it *was* some dream. That's the way it started out, right?" He picked up his head and fastened it on from the inside. Whatever illusion there had been in the shack had faded for me now, outside in the sunshine. They looked like some stragglers from a kids' costume party, suddenly foolish in the everyday street.

"Remember," said Keith. "We never tell anybody about this." He looked at Jim, and the silver head nodded.

"Never," said Jim, and then he snickered. He started back toward the shack.

"You shoulda known," Keith muttered to me, and I wondered if right here we were going to have it out. But he turned and followed Jim.

When we entered the shack, Harold was looking straight ahead.

"You've been in another part of the ship," he announced.

The three creatures stood in their configuration in front of him, and I went back to the radio.

"We'll take you back," said Jim. His voice was still mostly disguised, but he wasn't pausing. He just wanted this done with, and had stopped really trying.

Harold lowered his head. "Did I ask too many questions?" he asked. "Did I ruin it?"

"You did fine," said Jim, almost in his real voice.

Keith and Robby walked forward and put the blindfold on him again. We moved the chair around, but not as much. Our hearts were no longer in it.

We pushed him along through the woods, and he didn't say anything, and for that I had to thank him. As hard as he must have taken it, he didn't make it too hard for us.

We took him out to a field where we had poured some kerosene and lit it, to leave a large round blackened area. We wanted it to look like a place a spacecraft had landed. I don't know about the others, but I felt embarrassed when I saw it.

We left him there in the circle, with the blindfold on, his glasses in the weeds next to him. "Count to a hundred before you take it off," said Jim. Harold didn't say anything. After he removed the cloth, he'd be able to wander in practically any direction and he'd see houses.

We started walking away, but then Jim turned and went back toward Harold. He stopped when he was just a few feet away. For a moment again, it did seem eerie: this tall, silver-headed being looking down at the child. He was trying to sound like the creature again, but his own voice kept breaking through.

"*You can't think about you* . . . you and your parents
. . . that way. *No matter what they do.* It can make you . . .
nuts . . ." Then Jim moved away from him, and joined
the rest of us, and we walked away and didn't look
back.

SEVENTEEN

The rest of that day felt strange to me. My mother asked me how the paper drive had gone, and I said simply, "Fine." And then I sat in the living room and read the comics from the night before. But halfway through, I got up to see what they were doing. My father was out in the yard—I guess he really hated to be inside. He was snipping grass where it grew over into the dirt borders around the plants he had lined up on our property line. I asked him if there was anything I could do, and he thought for a moment and smiled a little and said that I could do some of the snipping, and that would free him to set up the hoses for watering the lawn. After I finished, I walked across the front grass and stood by him while he held the hose and sprinkled.

"I think I've almost got those thin spots filled in," he said.

"I'm really glad," I said.

After a while, I went in and sat in the living room

again. I tried to watch the hands move on the clock—but no matter how hard you looked, you could never see them move—you could only see the results of their having moved.

I went downstairs and asked my mother if I could help her sort out the wash. She said I could put all the dark socks in a pile. The dryer was whirling. She was humming to herself, putting white pieces of clothing together, and I just stood by her and put the brown and the black and the blue socks together, listening to the sound of the dryer.

When I finished with the socks, I said, "You know, when I was born. I mean, just before. Dad had just come back, he was pretty shaken up, they hadn't kept his job . . ."

She looked over at me. "What is it, Donald?"

"Oh," I said, "it's nothing. It's just that at school—we were reading about the baby boom. After the war, how everyone had kids."

"Of course," said my mother. "After something like that."

"But with Dad and all," I said. "It must have been a hard time."

She was putting the handkerchiefs and underwear together—behind us, the dryer was howling, like wind trapped in a tunnel. Then she paused. "Donald, I don't know what gets into you sometimes," she said.

"I don't know myself," I said, and shrugged. Then I turned and went upstairs, but still I saw her standing for a moment, deep in thought.

———

At dinner I kept imagining the others that night, eating at home with their parents. Robby fighting with his brothers and Keith telling his father how well he had done in the practice with the balls in the fog, how they came at you like major-league pitches and how one kid had even gotten a black eye; Jim with his mother at their little stand-up table in the same kitchen where that guy had drunk beers with her. And I thought about Harold: right now he was probably sitting at the table with his parents, and were they looking at each other over his head, or in quick glances when he looked away, edgy and resentful? But all the time he was watching, counting the months, catching the signals, like a boy with a lens gazing at flashes in a midnight sky.

Then I started asking about things. I got my father to talk about the yard, and my mother to talk about where she found the recipe for the ham we were eating, and then I said that with my birthday coming up—it was about three months away—I had some ideas of things I might be interested in this year, telescopes, and things like that. I thought you could get one pretty inexpensively.

"Not coins any longer?" asked my mother.

"Not so much," I said.

It all seemed to be going pretty well. But when we'd finished our lemon meringue pie and pushed our plates back, I heard Chief bark twice.

And then the rebel yell.

My mother looked at my father questioningly, but his thoughts seemed far away. After a moment, I said, "I better go see . . ."

They were in the back of our lot, shadowed in the trees.

"He's still there," said Jim. There was a funny kind of urgency in his voice I hadn't heard before.

"What do you mean?"

"He's still where we bloody left him," said Keith.

It was just the two of them; maybe Robby had trouble getting out, maybe his parents hadn't bought his story.

"I went back to check on him," said Jim. "I don't know why. He's still got that blindfold on. Then he takes it off, and stands up and looks around. Then he puts it on again. He stepped on his stupid glasses." I could see him shake his head in the twilight.

Chief made a kind of growling noise; he walked in a circle, his chain rattling, and then he lay down.

"He was supposed to find his way home," I said.

"Bright," said Keith.

I was still having a hard time understanding.

"He's *waiting*," said Jim. "For them—for us—to come back for him."

"Jesus Christ."

They didn't say anything, and I just heard my breath coming out short, thinking this was how it was, the barn had caught fire, what if there was someone inside . . .

"His parents aren't home yet," said Keith.

"Their house is still dark," added Jim. "But we don't know when they will get home. And if he's not there . . ."

"Maybe it will wake them up," I said sharply.

"They'll call the police," said Keith.

147

"Dammit," said Jim.

"We cleaned up things," said Keith. "We took back the cloaks and ripped them up. The silver heads, the balls, we just kicked them into the creek, and they went floating away."

"Yeah, great idea," said Jim. "They glow in the dark like goddam whatsit—comets or something."

"How were we to know?" said Keith. "Hey, wait. I just got an idea." He suddenly sounded to me like Robby. "What if we leave them a note—from Harold. That he ran away. Out to the woods. Then they'd find him."

"How're we going to write in his writing?" asked Jim. "Besides—he's in enough trouble already."

"He's not in any—" Keith started to say, and then stopped.

"I didn't expect this," I said.

"Bright guy," said Keith.

Lights suddenly came sweeping through the trees. A car was traveling down the street. We held our breath as it continued on its way—past Harold's house, past mine. It wasn't his parents, and it didn't suddenly erupt into flashing red signals and spot-lights, into the bloody lights . . .

"You're going to have to talk to him," Jim said to me.

I looked at them, and they were both staring back at me. In the darkness of my back yard, where their eyes should have been were just hollows, filled with shadow.

"Tell him whatever you have to—just get him to go home."

I nodded.

They turned and walked from me. As I headed toward my house, I felt a tight grip on my arm and a soft voice in my ear. "Don't tell him my name," said Keith. I pulled away from him: if he was going to get me back, it would be now. His face had that puffy look to it again, and then I saw that he—and Jim, too—were just scared kids, scared kids like Harold and me.

When I got back inside, my mother was doing the dishes, and my father was sitting at the kitchen table, smoking a cigarette. I sat down across from them, as if nothing had happened, and then I said suddenly, "That was Harold. He wants me to go over to his house."

My mother dried her hands on a towel and turned around. "Well, you can invite him here," she said.

I glanced at my father, through the smoke that was slowly spreading in front of him.

"I'd really like to go over there," I said.

The smoke was curling in front of my mother now, as well.

"He's got that telescope. He said it was a good night for stars." I paused. "It's just across the street," I said.

My mother and father were staring at me, without expression. Their faces were half hidden in the trails of smoke.

"All right, then," said my mother.

I followed the dim circle of light into the woods. I'd taken a flashlight from my room, but the batteries were low, and I thought if I were a Boy Scout this never would have happened. The pale yellow disk, with a black mark on it where the lens was cracked, shone onto trees and grass like a small moon, giving them momentary color. I heard sounds of small animals or birds skittering in the trees, and thought I saw the glint of some kind of eye.

I fell off the second rock I stepped on crossing the stream, and felt cold water course over my ankles. I stood there a moment until I got my balance. Then I crossed and clambered up the muddy wall on the far side.

The field where we dropped him was halfway to Wagoner Road. As I walked toward it, the trees thinned out, and I turned off the flash. I stepped through a patch of deadwood—branches cracking off when I brushed by them—and ahead I saw the cleared-out patch of grass. I stopped walking and ran my eyes over it, and then when I saw a shape I fixed on it. Harold was sitting with his legs drawn up, his arms around his legs. Out of the trees, I noticed for the first time that the sky above us was brilliant with stars: Arcturus, and Procyon, and Castor and Pollux.

I walked quietly toward him. His blindfold was off, and he was staring into the woods that started on the other side from where I was coming.

"Harold," I said softly, when I was about fifteen feet from him.

"Oh!" He turned around suddenly and squinted.

"It's Donald," I said, as I walked toward him. I could see that one of the arms of his glasses veered out away from his head, one of the lenses was cracked.

"Hi," he said sullenly.

"You should go home," I said.

He didn't make any move to get up.

"You know—" I started.

"I know," he said. "I really hate you." He looked down and then he started crying, and he reached over and started punching at me while he was sobbing, hitting at me wildly, as if he'd never learned to fight anyone.

I put up my hands to shield my face but let him hit me some on my shoulders and chest. "You son of a bitch," he kept saying, crying, and hitting me. "Son of a bitch. I hate you! I hate you!"

"I sort of do, too," I said.

He looked at me, and his mouth was drawn down. After a moment: "They wouldn't have used *kerosene*," he said fiercely. He threw some blackened weeds at me, and there was a faint odor to them. "They wouldn't have said, 'Count to a hundred and then you can look'—that's what a kid says. How stupid, you and whoever else your stupid friends were."

"You're right," I said.

"All because of your dog?" he asked angrily.

I wanted to say no one messes with me, but it seemed pointless, sitting in the field with this little kid.

He was silent, looking down at the ground.

"Their heads?" he said.

"Balls. Spray-painted."

"And some kind of radio?"

"Uh-huh."

"I can't see anything without my glasses."

I nodded.

"But the flying . . . "

"We just lifted you up in a chair," I said.

His shoulders slumped. "How stupid."

He looked down and shook his head. "I thought it for a while," he said. "And then I thought, if they are kids—and they somehow know this—I thought of you, then—maybe they're still not kids, too. Maybe they'd somehow been changed—into something else, into . . . beings from somewhere else. And that the kids didn't even know it themselves. That they'd been changed."

I was aware of the thousands of stars above us. "You mean, on the orders of a superior intelligence?"

"Something like that," he said.

"That's too creepy," I said.

He nodded, and then he bit his knuckle.

"I had really thought," he started, and then grew silent. He was blinking again, looking away from me. "I really do hate you," he said. He shook his head. "I didn't know what they would do, but I always knew what I'd do. I always thought I'd show them how to do things. They'd want to know . . . so much about us. They'd want to be . . . introduced." He smoothed down some of the grass in front of him with his hand. "They'd be a little scared, you see. They'd have so many questions, having shown up on a spaceship, from so far away. I had always thought I would be their guide. To all this." He looked up at the sky and then over at the dim shapes of the trees. "There would be nothing in the way of it. I'd have all kinds of time, nothing else I'd want to do more, not school or anything. I'd want to help them figure things out, how we eat plants and cows and how we breathe this oxygen-rich gas, and how we talk, with our lips and tongues, the words we say, the names we give to things. It would be the thing I'd want to do most, and they would know it . . ."

He was shaking his head, blinking, and then he looked over at me.

He started moving his hands.

"What is that?" I asked.

Together and apart, three fingers, a clenched fist, a V-for-victory sign, or maybe an L, a half circle like a C.

"It means 'Welcome,' he said. "It means I would welcome them to the planet." He wiped his eyes with his fingers.

"Welcome," I said softly. But with the stars and space above, and the burned-out circle surrounding us, it was as if it was we who had suddenly landed.

I stood up quickly. "We better get you home," I said.

It wasn't difficult to find the way. As we had planned, you didn't have to walk far in any direction to see houses, and we could see them now: lit-up back windows, with the families inside, yellow light if someone was reading, blue light if they were watching TV.

Harold's house was dark when we got to the patch of field behind it.

We started walking through his back yard. "One thing," I said. "I know how you feel . . . but I never asked. That day, that Friday, before this whole thing started. When you locked yourself in the car. How come you did that?"

It was as if he didn't hear me. He kept trudging ahead of me, toward the dark house—with the car still gone—and I suddenly knew.

153

The ball and bat were lying by the back walk. He began to climb up the stairs.

"I'll see you, Donald," he said.

I watched him get to the top step. He was just a little kid.

"Wait a second," I said.

He stopped and turned, and I already had the bat and ball in my hands. "I know it's kind of dark," I said. "But I could show you how to hit a few . . ."

He looked at me.

"Up to the stars," I said.

He seemed to think about that for a moment. Then he started down the steps.